Saving
Zoë

Saving Zoë

ALYSON NOËL

St. Martin's Griffin ❧ New York

SAVING ZOË. Copyright © 2007 by Alyson Noël. All rights reserved. Printed in the United States of America. For information, address St. Martin's Press, 175 Fifth Avenue, New York, N.Y. 10010.

www.stmartins.com

Library of Congress Cataloging-in-Publication Data

Noël, Alyson.
    Saving Zoë / Alyson Noël.—1st ed.
      p. cm.
    Summary: Instead of a fresh start, high school provides more grief and isolation to Echo, whose older sister died a year earlier, but insights gained from Zoë's diary—a fifteenth birthday gift from Zoë's boyfriend—about her sister's life and death change Echo in ways she could have never expected.
    ISBN-13: 978-0-312-35510-4
    ISBN-10: 0-312-35510-6
    1. Grief—Fiction. 2. Death—Fiction. 3. Sisters—Fiction. 4. Interpersonal relations—Fiction. 5. High schools—Fiction. 6. Schools—Fiction. I. Title.

PZ7.N67185 Sav 2007
[Fic]—dc22

2007017445

ISBN-13: 978-0-312-35510-4
ISBN-10: 0-312-35510-6

First Edition: September 2007

10   9   8   7

For my sisters, Jolaine and Dori, and in memory of
those who were taken too soon

Acknowledgments

I owe a huge debt of gratitude to: My readers, whose letters, e-mails, and posts to my bulletin board mean more to me than they probably realize; Kate Schafer, who believed in Echo's story and is everything I could want in an agent and more; everyone at St. Martin's Press, including but not limited to Matthew Shear, Jennifer Weis, Stefanie Lindskog, Anne Marie Tallberg, and Abbye Simkowitz, for their support; my father, who gets to my book signings early; and, as always, to Sandy, for everything.

One

They say there are five stages of grief:

1. Denial
2. Anger
3. Bargaining
4. Depression
5. Acceptance

Up until last year I didn't know there were lists like that. I had no idea people actually kept track of these things. But still, even if I had known, I never would've guessed that just a few days before my fourteenth birthday I'd be stuck in stage one.

But then you never think that kind of bad news will knock on your door. Because those kinds of stories, the kind that involve a stone-faced newscaster interrupting your favorite TV show to report a crucial piece of "late breaking news," are always about someone else's unfortunate family. They're never supposed to be about yours.

But what made it even worse is that I was the first to know.

Well, after the cops.

And, of course, Zoë.

Not to mention the freak who was responsible for the whole mess in the first place.

And even though they didn't exactly say anything other than "May we please speak to your parents?" It was the regret on those two detectives' faces, the defeat in their weary eyes, that pretty much gave it all away.

It was after school and I was home alone, trying to keep to my standard cookie-eating, TV-watching, homework-avoiding routine, even though I really couldn't concentrate on any of it. I mean, normally at 4:10 P.M. both my parents would still be at work, my sister, Zoë, would be out with her boyfriend, and I would be sitting cross-legged on the floor, wedged between the couch and the coffee table, dunking Oreos into a tall glass of cold milk until my teeth were all black, the milk was all sopped up, and my stomach was all swollen and queasy.

So I guess in a way I was just trying to emulate all of that, go through the motions, and pretend everything was normal. That my parents weren't really out searching for Zoë, and that I wasn't already in denial long before I had good reason to be.

But now, almost a year later, I can honestly say that I'm able to check off stages one through three, and am settling into stage five. Though sometimes, in the early morning hours, when the house is quiet and my parents are still asleep, I find myself regressing toward four. Especially now that September's here, putting us just days away from the one-year anniversary of the last time Zoë shimmied up the big oak tree, climbed onto my balcony, and came in through my unlocked french doors.

I remember rolling over and squinting against the morning light, watching as she pressed her index finger to her smiling lips, her short red nail like the bottom of an upside-down exclamation point, as she performed her exaggerated, cartoonish, stealth tiptoe through my room, out my door, and down the hall.

Sometimes now, when I think back on that day, I add a whole new scene. One where, instead of turning over and falling back to sleep, I say something important, something meaningful, something that would've let her know, beyond all doubt, just how much I loved and admired her.

But the truth is, I didn't say anything.

I mean, how was I supposed to know that was the last time I'd ever see her?

Two

When the woman at the funeral home, the one in the long floral dress, with the frizzy french braid, asked for a picture of Zoë, my mom dropped her head in her hands and sobbed so hysterically that my dad pulled her close, clenched his jaw, and nodded firmly, as though he was already working on it.

I stared at the toe of my black Converse sneaker, noticing how the fabric was wearing thin, and wondering what that lady could possibly need a picture for. I guess it seemed like a weird request, considering how pretty much everywhere you looked in our town you'd see a picture of Zoë. And since my sister was always so elusive and hard to pin down in life, it seemed like I actually saw more of her after her disappearance than I had when she lived down the hall.

First there were the two "missing person" flyers taped to just about every available surface. One a stiff, grainy, black-and-white grabbed in a panic and copied from last year's yearbook.

The other, one of Zoë's more recent headshots, depicting her as beautiful, loose, and happy, more like the sister I knew, that also included a generous reward for anyone with any information, no questions asked.

And then, as the days ticked by, her face started appearing just about everywhere—in newspapers, magazines, and nationally televised news reports. Even the makeshift memorial, built by well-wishers and propped up in front of our house, contained so many candles, poems, stuffed animals, angels, and photos of Zoë that it threatened to take over the entire street until my dad enlisted a neighbor's help and hauled it all away.

The funny thing was, Zoë had always dreamed of being a model, an actress, someone famous and admired by all. She longed for the day when she could escape our small, boring town, and go somewhere glamorous, like L.A., or New York, just someplace exciting and far from here. And so, while we were out searching, while we were busy smothering our doubt with hope, I played this kind of game in my head where I pretended that all of this was great exposure for Zoë and her future as a famous person. Like it was the ultimate casting call. And I spent those long, empty, thankless moments imagining how excited she'd be when she finally came home and saw her face plastered all across the nation.

But then later, in the mortuary, as I watched my parents make the world's most depressing arrangements, encouraged into credit card debt by the man in the stark black suit who guided them toward the most luxurious casket, the most abundant flowers, and the whitest doves—sparing no expense at her memory—I sat wide-eyed, realizing the lucrative business of loss, while wondering if my mom got the irony behind Zoë's ambition and the woman's request, and if that's why she was crying so hard.

But then, I guess there were millions of reasons to cry that day. So it's not like I had to go searching for The One.

I didn't know why that woman wanted a photo, but I doubted my dad, grief stricken and distracted, would ever remember to give her one. So after they'd signed away their savings and were headed out the door, I reached into my old blue nylon wallet, the one with the surf brand sticker still partially stuck to the front, its edges frayed and curled all around, and retrieved the photo Zoë had given me just a few weeks before, the one that showcased her large dark eyes, generous smile, high cheekbones, and long wavy, dark hair. The one she'd planned to send to the big New York and L.A. agencies.

"Here," I said, pressing it into the woman's soft, round hand, watching as she did the quick intake of breath I was so used to seeing when confronted with an image of Zoë for the very first time.

She looked at me and smiled, the fine lines around her blue eyes merging together until almost joining as one. "I'll be doing her makeup, and I want to get it just right. So, thank you—" She left that last part dangling, looking embarrassed that she knew all about my loss, but didn't know my name.

"Echo." I smiled. "My name is Echo. And you can keep the picture. Zoë would've liked that." Then I ran outside to catch up with my parents.

Three

Zoë and Echo are Greek names, even though we're not at all Greek. Zoë means life, and Echo, well, I know you know what it means, so I'll just say that it's also a nymph who pined away for some guy named Narcissus until nothing was left but her voice. Which is something, by the way, that I would never do. You know, fade away over some guy. I mean, not even Chess Williams, the cutest guy in my class since fourth grade, is worth crumbling for. Anyway, it's basically a Greek mythology thing, and I guess that's why we got names like that. Nothing to do with nationality, and everything to do with academics.

My parents are big on academics. Which I guess is why they're both professors. And, knowing I'll risk looking like a total brainiac nerd, I'll just go ahead and admit, right now and for the record, that I'm pretty big on academics too. But Zoë? Zoë hated all that. She was beautiful, and wild, and too busy getting into trouble and sneaking out of the house to ever slow down long enough to actually finish a book. Yet she was so sweet about it, and had such uncontained enthusiasm (for everything but homework), that no one ever held a grudge or judged her too harshly.

"Life is too exhilarating to read about! You gotta get out there and live it!" she'd say, just moments before sneaking onto my balcony and down the old oak tree, as I lay in bed reading one of my numerous library-issued novels.

But I'm nothing like Zoë. I'm average, not beautiful. I mean, my hair is medium brown and kind of limp, not rich and wavy like hers. And where she had amazing dark eyes with extra-thick long lashes, mine are light hazel, which may sound nice on paper, but believe me, they're far more functional than special. And my body, well, I'm really, really hoping that the years between fourteen and sixteen will be as kind and gener- ous to me as they were to her (though so far, I'm a couple weeks shy of fifteen and there's nothing to report). And I've definitely never been in any kind of trouble. Well, at least not the serious kind. I mean, so far my biggest offense is returning a library book two weeks late because I liked it so much I de- cided to read it again.

But Zoë? Well, let's just say that had she actually made it home that day, she would've been in for it big time.

"Echo?" my mom calls from the bottom of the stairs. "I'm leaving. Are you sure you don't need a ride?"

"Nope. Have a good day." I peek around my bedroom door, catching a quick glimpse of her as she heads outside be- fore locking all three dead bolts, even though I'll be leaving in less than two minutes.

But that's how we live now, overly cautious, verging on completely paranoid. And it took a solid fifty-five minutes of carefully argued debate, during last night's meatloaf, steamed asparagus, and garlic mashed potatoes dinner to get both of my parents to let me walk to school, as opposed to getting door-to-door service from one of them.

And it's not like I'm going it alone or anything, since all I have to do is go halfway down the block to my best friend Abby's, before we both stop on the corner to pick up our other best friend, Jenay.

Though I guess it's pretty much a miracle my mom decided to go back to teaching in the first place. I mean, right after everything happened she took a sabbatical so she could stay home and "look after me." I guess my parents blamed themselves for what happened. Thinking that their busy, working lives didn't allow for the kind of constant vigilance required to protect us.

But really, how much can you actually protect someone before it turns into imprisonment? Because just a few months into it, that's exactly how I started to feel, like a prisoner in my own home. I mean, at first I thought it would be nice to spend more time with my mom, especially after what we'd all just been through, but it didn't take long before she started acting more like a warden. And all she required of me was to go to school, come straight home, not to talk too much, and never to venture past the front door without:

> A valid reason and detailed explanation containing
> all of the whos, hows, whys, and wheres
> &
> an approximately exact ETA and ETD.

But none of that would've been so bad if I hadn't been so lonely. I mean, Abby and Jenay didn't come over nearly as much as you'd think. Mostly because their parents wouldn't let them, always mumbling some excuse about our family "needing our space during our difficult time." But I knew that wasn't the reason.

It's like when something really horrible and tragic happens, pretty much everyone starts giving you these sad, regretful looks as they slowly back away. Like our tragedy was contagious. Like our once warm and inviting home was now a place of darkness and doom, where extreme caution was clearly warranted.

So basically, all last year, when I wasn't at school, I was pretty much alone. I mean, my mom mostly stayed curled up on the couch, clad in her old blue terry cloth robe, staring blankly at the TV, tears pouring down her cheeks, while my dad lingered at work, staying later and later, and only rarely making it home before my bedtime.

And the weekends? Well, that's when they argued. Hurling accusations back and forth like blows in a boxing match, never tiring of their need to prove, once and for all, just who was more responsible for what happened to Zoë.

I used to think that tragedy brought people closer. But now, from everything I've experienced, I know it pretty much tears them apart.

Then again, all of that happened before my mom started taking her "happy pills," which enabled her to get off the couch, out of her robe, and back to work. The fighting stopped too. Only to be replaced with a flood of formality and excessive politeness, like we're all just strangers on a cruise ship, forced to eat our meals together, and act like we're interested.

And even though on the surface we seem to be doing better, the truth is my dad still "works" late, and my mom's eyes are more vacant than ever.

And as much as I miss Zoë, as much as my heart aches, as much as I'd do anything in the world just to get her back, there are times when I actually hate her too. Because this is what she's done to me. This is what she's left me with. Two broken, deeply suspicious, hollowed-out shells for parents, and the morbid curiosity of everyone I encounter.

Tucking my hair behind my ears, I grab my backpack, run down the stairs, lock all three locks, and head toward Abby's. But before I'm even halfway there, I see her heading toward me.

"Hey," she says, her long black ponytail swinging from side to side as her face breaks into a smile, exposing the blue metal braces she can't wait to get off, as her brown eyes squint against the sun.

"Am I late?" I ask, glancing at my watch, then back at her.

"I'm early. Aaron's driving me crazy, so I bailed," she says, shaking her head and rolling her eyes as we head toward the corner where we'll pick up Jenay. Abby's brother Aaron is two years younger and pretty much the bane of her otherwise extremely orderly existence.

"What's up with Aaron?" I ask.

"What *isn't* up with Aaron?" She shakes her head again. "He bugs me so bad, sometimes I wish he'd just disappear, never to return. Then I'd have some peace. I mean, just this morning—" Suddenly she stops walking, stops talking, and just stands there, gaping at me, her mouth hanging open, her brown eyes full of sorry and regret. "Oh God, I didn't mean—"

"It's okay," I say quickly, forcing my face to smile. "Seriously. So you were eating breakfast *and* . . ." I loop my arm through hers, leading her toward the corner, and hopefully away from her guilt. Everyone is always apologizing to me now, and sometimes I wonder if it will ever stop.

"*And* there's Jenay," she says, deftly changing the subject. "Omigod, are those—? Oh man, she is *so* lucky! How did she talk her stepmom into buying those jeans? *How?*"

"Hey, you guys," Jenay says, leaning in to give each of us a hug.

But Abby's strictly business, determined to gather the facts. "I need details," she says. "*How* did you get those? *What* did you do? And will it work on my mom too?" she asks, slowly circling Jenay, her eyes coming to rest on those telltale designer back pockets, the ones with the gold embroidery that makes the whole $220 price tag seem worth it.

"Well, if you promise to get straight As, babysit my little brother every Saturday night for the rest of your life, and remain a virgin until you're old and gray, then maybe she'll get you a pair too." Jenay laughs.

"Call me when you've got that whole potty training thing handled. The last thing I need is another squirt in the eye," Abby says, maneuvering herself into the center, looping her arms through ours, and leading us toward school.

Since Abby, Jenay, and I don't share any classes, this is the last time we'll see each other until the ten-minute break between second and third periods. Which, even though technically it's only two hours away, I have to admit that right now it feels like forever.

"Okay, so everyone remembers where to go, right?" Abby asks, having deemed herself our group leader sometime back in early elementary school, when Jenay and I were too oblivious to argue or engage in any kind of power struggle.

I nod and gaze nervously around campus, as Jenay laughs. "Yes, Mom." She smiles.

"Okay, and remember, you can totally text me if you need anything. Because I'm leaving my cell on vibrate," Abby adds.

And even though I'm gazing across campus at Marc—who up until last week I hadn't seen for nearly a year—I'm fully aware of Abby's stare and how that last part was meant for me.

If you were going to categorize us, and let's face it, most people just naturally do, you could say that Jenay is the clumsy, funny, pretty one (even though most of the time she doesn't know it), Abby's the super-organized, bossy one (and yeah, most of the time she does know it), and I'm the completely tragic one. Though before last year, most people probably would've said that I'm the cynical, brainy one. But that doesn't mean that Jenay's not smart, or that Abby's not pretty, or that I can't be hopeful. Those are just the things that people usually notice first. But since Abby and Jenay have been my best friends for as long as I can remember, I guess I don't really see them that way. When I look at them I just see two people who are always there for me, who can always make me laugh, and who can sometimes even help me forget.

Clutching my schedule, I recheck my room number, even though it's practically tattooed on my brain, ever since the "dry run" Abby subjected us to a little over a week ago, so we wouldn't look like "your typical clueless freshmen" (even though we were) on our very first day.

"They're here. The schedules. Check your mailbox and meet me on the corner in five," she'd said, as I slipped on some flip-flops and fled out the door, thankful that my mom was out running errands, which spared me the usual detailed explanations.

When I got to the corner, Jenay was already waiting, her long blond hair flowing loose around her shoulders, as her fingers picked at the hems of her layered blue and white tank tops.

"Hey," she said, gazing up and smiling, her blue eyes squinting against the sun. "Abby forgot her cell so she ran back to get it."

"Why?" I asked.

But Jenay just shrugged. "You know Abby," she said, reaching for my schedule. "Damn. Once again, no classes together. Well that's what you get for being so smart." She laughed, returning the yellow slip of paper and getting back to her double frayed hems.

I just stood there, not saying a word, since I never really know what to say when she gets all self-effacing like that. But then Abby ran up, waving her phone, as evidence of her mission accomplished, and led us on the three-and-a-half-block trek to our future home away from home for the next four years—Bella Vista High. Go Bobcats.

Having grown up in this town, it's not like I hadn't already been there like a zillion times before, not to mention how it's the same school Zoë went to right up until the first month of her junior year. But still, every time I approached that concrete slab of a campus I couldn't help but wonder just exactly what those founders were thinking when they named it Bella Vista. Because as far as beautiful views went, well, there weren't any.

We navigated our way around, located our lockers (which thankfully weren't all that far apart), and decided where we'd meet on our ten-minute break (Abby's locker), and then again at lunch (Abby's locker—until we secured a more solid place). And after we'd memorized all of our room numbers and their corresponding locations, we headed back home, with Jenay doing an impersonation of Ashlee Simpson that had me bent over laughing the entire way.

Well, until I saw Marc.

I stopped midstride, just stood there and stared. Noticing how his shoulders slumped low, how his dark eyes stayed guarded, and how each drag of his cigarette seemed filled with intent, like he was meant to be sitting on the hood of his car, just outside the Circle K, at precisely that moment. But just as he lifted his head and his eyes fixed on mine, Abby and Jenay each grabbed an arm, pulling me away from him and closer to the safety of home.

But now, having just seen him again, I realize this will probably become like a daily occurrence. And I can't believe I didn't grasp that before. I mean, even though I don't share the same opinion of him as most people in this town, having to go to the same school with him just totally sucks. Because now it's like there's no safe place, nowhere I can just be me without the constant shadow of Zoë. No place where I can start fresh and try to move on.

Four

Even though it probably seems like Abby would've been the one to secure the good lunch table, it was Jenay who succeeded. Because in the world of cafeteria real estate, long blond hair, big blue eyes, a great smile, and a nicely filled out snug white T-shirt trumps the best laid plans of a future life coach every single time.

"It must be the jeans. They're magic, that's why they cost so damn much," Abby says, sliding in next to Jenay and gawking at Chess Williams and the almost equally cute Parker Hendricks, who are sitting just mere inches away.

But Jenay just shakes her head and laughs. "Don't forget that they've just been demoted to lowly freshmen in a sea of hot seniors. So technically, they're lucky to be sitting by *us*," she whispers, smiling triumphantly.

I slide onto the end of the bench and unzip my lunch pack, curious to see what's inside, and hoping it's not the dreaded leftover meatloaf sandwich that only my mom could view as a logical choice. I mean, for someone with an I.Q. ranked firmly among genius, who makes her living as an academic (aka professional smart person), she just can't seem to grasp the fact that some leftovers were never meant for cafeteria consumption or any other lunchtime scenario that doesn't entail complete privacy, a bib, and the luxury of eating over a sink. But as I unzip the top and peek inside, I'm relieved to see the unmistakable tubelike shape of my favorite deli wrap sandwich and not a white bread monstrosity dripping with meat juice on my very first day.

I tear open my chips and fish one out, pretending not to notice how just about every single Bella Vista student sitting within a two-mile radius is totally staring at me. I mean, if I thought things were a little rough this morning in Honors English, American History, Geometry, and French, well, most of my fellow classmates went to school with me last year too, which means they've pretty much gotten an eyeful ever since it all began. But now, being surrounded by all of these people who used to know Zoë, who were friends with Zoë, or who, now that she's gone, like to pretend they were friends with Zoë, makes me feel completely naked and exposed. Like a regretful "life art" model being stared at and scrutinized as everyone takes it all in, draws it all down, and interprets everything they see in their own biased way.

And even though I kind of expected this, that doesn't mean I can actually handle it. And there's just no way I can finish my lunch with everyone whispering, pointing, and gawking.

So just as Jenay starts talking to Chess, so casually and easily you'd think she'd been at it for years, and Abby scoots even closer to Parker—who she's secretly crushed on forever—I rise from the table and move for the door, hoping I can make it safely inside the bathroom before I start hurling.

It's weird how you can hire a bodyguard to protect you from physical harm, yet there's no one who can keep you from emotional harm. And as great as my friends have been, doing their best to shield me from everything they can, there's just no way they can defend me from all of the prying eyes, pointed fingers, and loudly whispered, *"Omigod! That's her! You know, the little sister,"* that follows me wherever I go.

I push into the empty bathroom, dump the contents of my lunch pack into the big green trash can against the far wall, then run cold water over my hands until the nausea passes. Then I smooth my hair, straighten my shirt, and head right back outside, and straight into Marc.

"Echo," he says, his dark brown eyes peering into mine, as his pale slim hands clasp nervously at his sides. Up close, he seems thinner, and his hair looks darker, hanging long and loose around his angular face. But he's still amazing, only different. Less contrived, more authentic, yet also kind of lost.

I just stand there, smelling the nicotine wafting off of him, remembering how it was Zoë who got him started.

And just as he opens his mouth to speak, Abby runs up and grabs hold of my shirt. "Echo! Hey! Let's go," she says, tugging on my sleeve and pulling me away.

Five

Every day gets a little easier. But not because the whispering stops, or the staring ceases, or the teachers stop giving me that "Oh, you poor sad thing" look. Nope, all of that remains as blatant as ever. The reason things are getting easier is because every day I get a little better at ignoring it. It's like, if no one else is willing to change, then I'll be the one who does. So, I've simply stopped reacting. I mean, now, when people whisper as I pass in the hall, I refuse to hear it. And when my English teacher gives me *that look,* I avert my eyes. And when I walk through the cafeteria and everyone stops eating and talking so they can point and stare, I absolutely refuse to care. I just focus on eating my sandwich, drinking my Snapple, and watching Jenay flirt with Chess.

"Omigod, do you think he'll ask you to homecoming?" Abby asks, just seconds after the lunch bell rings and Chess and Parker head for class.

But Jenay just gazes down at the ground, blushing and shrugging like she hasn't even considered it.

"Homecoming? Jeez, I haven't even thought about going," I say, walking alongside them and gazing at Jenay, knowing that in a race between the three of us, she's definitely the best bet. I mean, the odds are pretty much against a trifecta, at least with me in the race, and since Abby's also like me, and has no idea how to flirt, I'm placing my wager on Jenay, for win, place, and show.

"He likes you, anyone can tell," Abby says, smiling when she sees her blush.

But Jenay just shrugs. "Well, I guess we'll just see what happens next weekend then, won't we?" she says, waving over her shoulder and heading toward class.

"What's going on next weekend?" I ask, searching Abby's face, wondering what they could possibly be keeping from me.

But she just shrugs. "You know Jenay." She laughs, bringing her finger to her temple and making the universal sign for looney toons. "See you after school?"

"Not today," I say, watching her go and wondering if she heard me.

After school I have an appointment with a shrink. Though I guess when most people are seeing someone like that they usually say "my shrink." As in, "after school I have an appointment with MY shrink." But I don't like to think of him like that. I mean, I can barely stand the guy, so I certainly don't want to think of him as *mine.*

Besides, it's not like I see him all that often anymore. And it's not like he actually ever helped me when I did. I mean, okay, so this completely horrible thing happened to my family. I still can't see how sitting in his office and sobbing my eyes out to the tune of $150 for a fifty-minute hour is ever going to benefit anyone other than *him*.

But my parents, being intellectually minded, called on their most sought-after colleague, who, according to my mom, actually gets away with charging twice that amount, and who "out of kindness, compassion, and as a huge favor to our family has decided to give us a deeply discounted rate."

So because of all that, I was pretty much forced to spend every Tuesday after school, for almost my entire eighth grade year, sitting on that brown leather couch, with a beige floral Kleenex box placed squarely before me, as the Dr. Phil wannabe tried to trick me into saying the *actual words*, to *verbalize* and not *euphemize* what really happened to Zoë.

But even though I like to read and write, and even though I really do believe that words do hold the power to harm or heal, this was just one of those cases where words didn't seem all that important. And no way was I giving in, just so he could feel all smug and accomplished and like he just might actually know what he's doing.

But since I haven't been to see him since the beginning of last summer, today is supposed to serve as some sort of checkup or progress report or something. I guess since it also happens to be the one-year anniversary of Zoë's disappearance, my parents figured it was a good idea to have me stop by and pay the good doctor a little fifty-minute visit.

"Echo, come in. How've you been?" he asks, as I slide onto the familiar brown couch, eyeing the strategically placed tissues.

"I'm okay." I shrug, gazing around the room, noticing how some of the artwork has changed but knowing better than to mention it. I mean, these people analyze everything you do, from the moment you arrive to the moment you leave, so extreme caution is advised.

"How's school?" he asks, gazing at me through the upper

part of his glasses, like he thinks wearing them down around the tip of his nose makes him look smarter or something.

"Fine." I cross my legs and fold my hands in my lap, but then I immediately undo it since I don't want him to think I'm feeling anything other than totally relaxed, happy-go-lucky, and free.

"How are your classes, your teachers?"

"Good, and good," I say, cracking a smile so he'll know just how light and breezy I'm feeling today.

"And your friends? Still hanging around with those two girls?"

"Yup, pretty much since the beginning of time," I tell him, gazing at his bald head and pathetic goatee, and wondering why he can't see the oh so obvious symbolism in *that*.

"Any boyfriends?" He smiles gently.

But I refuse to answer. He's always pushing me to talk about boys and sex and stuff. But instead, I just give him a baleful look.

"Zoë always had lots of friends and boyfriends." He says that like he used to hang out with her or something. Like he knew her really well, better than me.

"Yeah? Well, I'm not Zoë, am I?" I fold my arms across my chest, even though I know full well that he's only trying to bait me. "And even though she may have had a lot of friends, she only had *one* boyfriend," I say, wondering just how crazy you have to be to pay three hundred dollars for fifty minutes of *this*.

"Are you still angry with Zoë?" He leans back in his chair and crosses his legs, causing me to catch an unfortunate glimpse of his brown argyle socks and flaky white shin that is almost as bald as his head.

"Why would I be angry with Zoë? She was my *friend,* and my *sister,* and I *loved* her." I roll my eyes, shake my head, and focus hard on my watch.

He sits there, watching me carefully, not saying a word. But I'm not buying it. This is just another one of his traps. I mean, I watch enough TV crime dramas, and I've read enough thrillers to know that cops, journalists, shrinks—they all rely on the same lame tricks. They all worship the power of the long penetrating stare and lingering silence that practically never fails in getting their suspect to divulge all of the personal, private information they never intended to spill.

But unlike most people, I'm not afraid of silence. And I couldn't care less about being stared at. In fact, I've grown so used to it that it doesn't even faze me.

So we sit. Him staring at me. Me staring at my watch. Seeing the second hand go round and round, knowing that each silent minute is costing my parents another three bucks.

And when our time is finally up, he looks at me and says, "Echo, are you ready to talk about Zoë?"

But I just grab my backpack and head out the door. "Zoë's gone," I tell him, closing it firmly behind me.

Six

My friends are acting weird. And if I didn't know better, if I was the more paranoid type, I would probably start to wonder if they still wanted to be my friends. But since we walk to school together every day, meet at break, sit together at lunch, and then walk all the way home again, it's not like they're trying to ditch me. It's more like they're trying to keep a secret from me. One that Jenay almost keeps giving away, which causes Abby to glare at her with narrowed eyes and a shaking head. I mean, I don't know what they're up to, but it definitely has something to do with this weekend.

"So, any b-day plans?" Abby asks, slipping her arm through the strap on her bag and hoisting it onto her shoulder.

I gaze at the ground, retracing the steps toward home, while remembering my last birthday, which, having fallen right in the middle of all the Zoë stuff, was hardly worth celebrating. And I seriously doubt this year will be any better. I mean, from here on out, every time I make it to another year, it will only remind me of how Zoë *didn't*. And tell me, where's the "Happy" in that?

But I don't want to share that with my friends and drag them down too, so instead I just go, "I don't know. We'll probably go to dinner or something." I shrug. "Though my mom did promise to bake my favorite cake, so if you guys wanna come over after, it's probably okay."

"Pineapple upside-down?" Jenay asks, her eyes lighting up as she smiles.

"No, that's *your* favorite. Mine's red velvet." I adjust my backpack, redistributing the weight so I won't end up all lopsided and bent when I'm old.

"I *love* red velvet. Just give me a time and I'm there." Abby smiles.

"I don't know, eight, eight thirty?" I say, glancing up just in time to catch them exchanging a secret look.

The second I slip my key in the door, my cell phone rings. And I freeze, trying to decide which is more important, turning the key and beginning the long process of getting inside, or answering my phone. Because with two more dead bolts and a knob lock to go, there's just no way I can accomplish both.

I heave a loud sigh, drop my bag, and ransack through the books and papers as I search for my cell. And by the time I find it, it's almost too late, so instead of checking ID I head straight for hello.

"Echo?" The voice is definitely male but decidedly unfamiliar. I mean, the only male that ever calls is my dad.

"Yeah?" I mumble, curious who it could be.

"It's me. Marc."

"Oh." I just stand there, clutching the phone, wondering what he wants. I mean, after that first day at school, I've definitely seen him a few more times, but it's not like we stop and talk. But then, nobody talks to Marc anymore. And even though that makes me feel pretty sad on his behalf, that doesn't mean I want to talk to him either.

"I know this is weird, but I was kind of hoping I could see you," he says.

I gaze at the driveway and the long crack that runs down the center, as I search for a way out. "Oh, I don't know. I mean, I'm kind of busy and all," I finally say, cringing at how false that sounds.

"Listen, I know it's awkward. And I know how your parents don't want me around. But I also know that tomorrow's your birthday, and I have something for you, something I think you're gonna like. So, how 'bout it? Will you meet me?"

I hesitate, gripping the phone and weighing my options. Then I hoist my bag onto my shoulder, slide my key out of the lock, and go, "Where should we meet?"

There's this lake in a park not far from my house that I always used to go to as a kid. Even though it's not the kind of lake you'd ever want to swim in, since the water is murky and polluted and full of Big Gulp cups and beer cans floating along the top like they have every right to be there. I mean, someone would pretty much have to hate you to actually throw you in. But still, every weekend, people show up by the dozens, toting picnic baskets and spreading out towels, eager to spend the day lazing around, gazing at the scenery, and pretending they're somewhere better. And even though I used to like to do that too, heading there now reminds me of just how long it's been.

I see him sitting by the water's edge just before he sees me. And even though I hate to admit it, my first instinct is to bolt. To just take off running, as fast and far as I can, as though my very life depends on it. But since I'm pretty sure he doesn't deserve that, I force myself to keep putting one foot in front of the other until I'm standing directly before him.

"You made it," he says, his smile like a question mark, his eyes more unsure than I ever could've imagined.

I stand there and shrug. Then drop my bag and sit down beside him.

"Zoë and I used to come here all the time," he says, dipping his hand into a bag full of Wonder bread, tossing fat handfuls to a flock of greedy ducks. "She used to feed them so much, I teased her about making them obese, and inflicting them with type two diabetes. But she'd just laugh and say she was trying to build trust, so that someday they'd come waddling up and eat the crumbs right out of her hand."

I glance at him briefly, wondering if his eyes will fill with tears. But when he turns to me and smiles, I know he's beyond all that, having moved his way through the grief list, and is now settled in some other place.

"How are you?" he asks, searching my face.

"Okay." I avert my eyes toward the ducks, but nod so he'll believe it. I know he has something to give me, something to tell me, but my heart is pounding so hard and my palms are growing so sweaty, I'm pretty sure I no longer want it.

We sit like that for a while, him feeding the ducks, me nervous and freaked. Then he shakes his head, turns to me, and says, "Thanks for coming. I know it's probably weird for you, but it really is important. So, well, here." He reaches into the old khaki schoolbag, the one he's always lugging around, then hands me a small leather-bound book, the cover bearing a cobalt so rich and blue, I immediately think of Zoë.

"What's this?" I ask, rubbing my fingers over the smooth soft leather, the same shade of blue as her walls.

"Her diary." He looks right at me, his dark eyes intense and no longer blinking. "It was in her backpack. The one she left with me that day, the day she—" He stops and shakes his head. "Anyway, it's hers and it's personal, and I didn't want the cops to get their hands on it because there's nothing in there that would've helped them, nothing they didn't already know. Not to mention how it's none of their business. And I didn't want your parents to see it since there's stuff in there that she never wanted them to see. So I kept it. I've had it this whole time. But now I want you to have it." He sees the look on my face and raises his right hand, like he's on a witness stand. "I gave them everything else, though, I swear."

I hold the book with both hands, too shaky and scared to peek. "Why me?" I ask, still gazing at the cover. "I mean, why don't you just keep it?"

"I think you should know her," he says, his eyes fixed on mine.

"But I *did* know her! And I *do* know her!" I grab my backpack and stand up quickly, wanting nothing more than to get away.

"You didn't know her like that. You didn't know the whole person," he says, his face solid and set, like he's just so sure about everything he's saying.

"Did *you* read it?" I ask, my hands shaky, watching as he nods in answer.

I stand there, taking him in, the lean build, the longish hair, the black T-shirt, the faded jeans, the chiseled face with the most amazing dark eyes. "You're not supposed to read other people's diaries," I say, turning away and running toward home.

Seven

The second I hear "Surprise!" I feel like an idiot. I mean, thinking back on Jenay's inability to keep a secret, and Abby's oh-so-obvious attempts to cover, it's pretty clear I should've known from the start. But after last year's birthday, when the only candles I was asked to blow out were for Zoë's candlelight vigil, my expectations for any future celebrations were at an all-time low.

"Were you surprised?" Jenay and Abby ask, obviously delighted at being able to pull it off so successfully.

"Totally," I say, slipping out of my favorite navy blue peacoat and gazing at all the decorations: the purple, orange, and pink paper lanterns; the matching candles, floor pillows, and balloons; not to mention the big red velvet cake pierced in the center with fifteen pink candles that my mom must have dropped off when I was bogged down in homework.

"So I guess you don't really need this after all?" I say, smiling as I hold up the dog-eared copy of *Le Petit Prince,* which is not only required reading for French I, but also Jenay's excuse for luring me over.

But she just laughs as she leads me deeper into the room.

I'm surprised by how crowded it is. And even though I smile and wave and say hi to all of these people I recognize from school, if you tried to test me, pop quiz me on their names, the truth is I'd totally fail. I mean, just because they came doesn't mean I actually know them. And it feels like one of those episodes of *Friends,* where they throw a party and all of these extras show up. All of these supposed *other* good friends, lounging on that famous TV couch, talking and laughing and sharing the screen, like they've been there all along and you just hadn't noticed.

And even though I'd like to believe that all of these people are here to see me, the truth is I know it's because of Abby and Jenay. They're the ones who invited them. They're the ones who've gone out of their way to know them.

Abby runs off to get me a drink as I squeeze into a narrow space on the end of the couch, smiling awkwardly at the girl sitting beside me, who turns to me and says, "Omigod, you should've seen your face when you first walked in! You looked so surprised, like you'd just seen a ghost!"

Then I watch as her face freezes in horror, just seconds after realizing what she really just said.

But I just launch straight into my well-honed "damage control" routine. The one where I smile and nod and give a friendly look, one that hopefully conveys the message: *as far as I'm concerned you have nothing to feel bad about.* Then I get up off the couch and mumble something about needing to go help Abby.

And as I'm walking away I hear her friend say, "Omigod, I can't believe you just said that! Hello? Remember what happened to her sister?"

Eventually it's gotta stop, right? The way people look at

me. The way they treat me. The way everyone around me goes out of their way to avoid certain words in my presence. As though the mere sound of *missing, vanished, Internet predator, gone, lost,* or *disappeared* will somehow reduce me to tears.

I know she meant well. I know she was only trying to make conversation with me, a girl whose party she's at and yet barely knows. But how can I ever be friends with someone who can't see me as anything other than Tragedy Girl?

How can I hang with people who refuse to see that despite the whole thing with my sister, I'm really not so different from them?

How can I make new friends when everyone feels so uncomfortable and guarded around me all the time?

I mean, right after the whole thing with Zoë, I became hugely, insanely popular. All of these kids who'd barely spoken to me before started lining up in hopes of being my new best friend. But even though at first I kind of liked all of the attention, it didn't take long to figure out how most of them were just voyeurs. Just a bunch of tragedy whores who wanted to get close to me so they could report back to the others. As though their social standing would somehow elevate once they told the story of how they went for ice cream with the sister of the girl who got . . .

Anyway, I learned pretty quick how to spot those people a mile away. And Abby and Jenay wasted no time in forming a tight, secure shield, protecting me from any and all future fake friendship attempts.

But now that we're in high school, it's obvious they want to branch out, meet new people, expand their horizons, whatever. And it's not that I blame them, or would ever try to stop them. I'm actually more worried about holding them back.

Or even worse, attracting all the wrong people, like the sideshow circus freak that I am.

"Here's the birthday girl," Jenay says, acting all giddy,

even though I'm 100 percent certain the only thing occupying her cup is crushed ice and Sprite.

Abby hands me my drink and sits on the couch, as Parker scootches away from her so he can make room for me. "Have a seat," he says, smiling and patting the free space beside him.

I glance at Abby wondering if she minds, then squeeze in beside Parker, thinking how weird it feels to be doing that considering how long I've known him, and how that's the first time he's ever scooted anywhere for me. But then again, the only time he ever spoke to me before was to say, "Sorry" as he fetched a soccer ball he'd just accidentally kicked at my head.

But I guess that's because Parker always hangs with Chess, and Chess always hangs with the popular crowd. And even though our junior high was just as cliqued up as any other school, and even though Abby, Jenay, and I have never been part of that über-cool group, we somehow managed to get out of there pretty much unscathed, avoiding a big, dramatic, *Mean Girls* showdown, which left us with a clean slate and no grudges to carry over into high school.

But now, with Parker making room for me, I realize Jenay was right about them being demoted, as most of the girls from their old group have already moved on, setting their sights on all the hot sophomores, juniors, and seniors. Which pretty much leaves the pick of the freshman litter for the rest of us to browse.

"We should play spin the bottle," Chess says, his eyes darting among us, looking to see who, if any, will bite.

"Why not seven minutes in Heaven?" Parker says, laughing and high-fiving Chess.

"Um, when did my party become a Judy Blume book?" I ask, hoping and praying that they're not at all serious.

"I think it sounds kind of fun," Jenay says, looking at me with eyes that are practically begging me to lighten up. "You know, retro." She smiles.

Retro for who? I think, since neither she, I, nor Abby has ever played this game before. Remember what I said about not being cool? Well, that means we weren't invited to any of the cool parties either. But since it's obvious she just wants an excuse to kiss Chess, and since I don't want to be the one who gets in her way, I just shrug and act like I really don't care.

Then Teresa, the alpha girl who held the top junior high royalty position solidly through both seventh and eighth grades, and who's now decided to join our meager group (probably because her original group disbanded and she'd rather be a big fish in our tiny little pond than a guppy in an ocean of upperclassmen), rolls her eyes and says, "Please, those games are so juvenile."

"But I just saw Carrie play it on *Sex and the City*," Jenay says, her voice sounding as pouty as her face looks.

"Again, *over! Syndication!*" Teresa shakes her head as she digs through her purse, having positioned herself on the rug near our feet. "I mean, if you guys want to make out with someone then just make out. Get over it already, because nobody cares." She pulls a vodka mini from her bag and unscrews the cap. "Anybody?" she asks, holding it up in offering.

I glance at Jenay and it's clear that she's torn. Partly pissed that Teresa's taking over the party, yet partly wondering if she should maybe just relax and let her. I mean, the fact that Teresa deigned to show up probably feels like a major coup.

"None for me," Abby says, leaning back against the cushions and narrowing her eyes at this new, bossy intruder.

"Ditto," I say as a show of support, even though I do kind of want some, just to see what it's like.

And when I look over at Jenay, waiting for her to chime in, she just shrugs and holds up her cup, pushing it toward Teresa.

Apparently Teresa's dad is a frequent flyer, which basically means she's got a purse full of airplane minis. And with pretty much everyone drinking (except Abby and me), and the lights turned low, and the music turned up, Parker leans in and whispers, "Wanna take a walk?"

I glance over at Jenay and Chess, who are totally making out right in front of us, then I squint at Parker and go, "Where? I mean, Jenay's parents are upstairs so we really shouldn't leave the basement."

But he just smiles. "I know a place," he says, standing before me and offering his hand.

And even though it sounds totally fishy to me, I still get up and follow.

When I think of coat closets, I usually think of itchy wool and cloying mothballs. But that's only because I don't have three brothers. Because from the moment I stepped inside there's been a hockey stick wedged against my butt, and it's accompanied by the most gag-worthy smell of B.O. I've ever encountered. Though I'm sure it's not coming from Parker since I don't remember him ever smelling bad, not to mention how this entire time, both his hands have been wrapped loosely around my waist and haven't wandered anywhere near my butt.

"Have you ever done this before?" he whispers, pulling me close.

I squint into the dark space before me, trying to make out the blondishness of his hair, the bluishness of his eyes, and the overall cuteness of his face that's kept him solidly in the number two position, directly beneath Chess, on the "cutest boys in school" list we've been keeping since fourth grade. But all I can make out is the vague outline of his head, and I wonder if he's asking if I've ever been in this closet before, or if I've ever kissed a guy before. Because to be honest, that wasn't exactly clear. But still, I guess the answer to both of those questions is pretty much the same, no and no. So that's what I tell him.

"Are you sure you're okay with this?" he asks, his voice filled with so much sweetness and concern that I'm shocked. Because honestly, I thought he'd be in full grope mode by now. "I mean, you're so nice. And I like you. So I don't want to push or anything."

I'd give anything to see his face right now, because this is not at all the cocky, loud, overconfident Parker from the lunch table, the one I assumed I'd be wrestling with. And the truth is, whether he actually kisses me or not really doesn't matter. I mean, I feel pretty neutral about the whole thing. I'm more surprised by the fact of how he even *wants* to kiss me. And how he's being so nice. And how he just said he *likes me!*

And I know I probably shouldn't waste this opportunity since things like this never happen to me, and because of that, this could be my one and only shot at a normal adolescent experience. But still, I can't help but ask, "Did you just say you like me?" I know it's lame and insecure, but I need a little clarification, 'cause to be honest, this is pretty hard to believe.

"Yeah. I think you're really cute, and nice, and stuff. Always have. You just never seemed very interested," he says.

I know I should probably be satisfied with that, and just shut up and let him kiss me already, but I really need to get to the bottom of this. So I go, "Seriously?"

"Seriously." He laughs. "But it's like, you and Jenay and Abby were always so tight that I guess I was too shy to try to break in."

"You're shy?" I say, unable to keep my disbelief in check.

"Yeah, but I'm working on it," he says, pulling me even closer. "So, is it okay? Can I kiss you now?"

I kind of wish he hadn't asked, 'cause it makes me feel really awkward to give him permission. But still, I guess it's better than never being asked, and possibly never being kissed. So I just nod and go, "Um, okay."

So he does. He leans in and kisses me. First he does it with his mouth closed. Then with it slightly open. And at one point he even slips his tongue in for a little bit. Then he pulls away, and says, "Was that okay?"

I nod. But then I remember how dark it is, which means he probably couldn't see that, so I clear my throat and say, "Um, yeah, it was nice."

And that's when he does it again.

Eight

By the time I get home, the house is mostly dark. And as I tiptoe upstairs and peek into their room, I'm surprised to find my parents already asleep. I mean, normally, well, I guess *normally* I don't go to parties, but still, for the last year, every time I left the house unchaperoned, I always returned to blazing lights, a flickering TV, and at least one, if not both, of my parents staying up late, playing night sentinel.

But maybe this is a good sign. Maybe things are finally looking up. Maybe my parents' paranoid period is coming to an end. Or maybe, this is just the result of my mom's addiction to happy pills, and my dad's utter exhaustion.

I change out of my clothes and slip into my pink-and-white striped pajamas, then I pad into the bathroom to brush my teeth and wash my face of what little makeup I bothered to wear. And as I peer at my reflection, I lean closer to the mirror, noticing how my lips are all red and swollen, and my cheeks all flushed and tender, and I watch them grow even redder when I realize it's because of Parker.

I guess I just never imagined something like that would happen to me. I mean, don't get me wrong, it's not like I planned to join a nunnery, or take a vow of celibacy, or anything crazy like that. Heck, I even assumed I'd get married someday, giving birth to the requisite number of kids. But all of that seemed so distant and far away. Like it was just one more thing on life's big "To Do" list. Just stuff that grownups did, like subscribing to a newspaper or paying bills.

I guess I never thought about the whole *attracting* part of it. And how I might feel about someone. And how they might feel about me.

And it's not like I'm hideous or anything. I mean, I'm pretty much your basic, all-American, standard issue girl. But still, it's not like I'm fun and sparkly like Jenay. And I'm certainly not amazing like Zoë. So I guess that's why it's hard for me to make sense of that kiss. And how afterward, Parker stuck by me for the rest of the night.

When I wake up soaked in sweat at 3:06 A.M., feeling panicky, with my face all wet and my throat all tight and sore as though I've been sobbing in my sleep, I force myself to just lay there, slowly breathing in and out as I count, starting at one hundred and working my way down, just like that shrink suggested that time I accidentally told him about my dreams.

But even after counting, even after changing out of my damp pajamas and into clean dry ones, even after drinking a glass of water and assuring myself that there's absolutely no reason to panic, I still can't seem to relax enough to fall back to sleep. And then I make it even worse when I start thinking about my party, and how everything's changing so fast in a way I once anticipated, only now that it's happening, I'm no longer so sure.

I mean, my parents didn't wait up, and a boy actually *wanted* to kiss me. And even though at the beginning of the night those two things would've sounded amazingly cool, now at o dark thirty, they no longer do.

Because, let's face it, there's comfort in being cautious. And there's peace in the predictable.

But now, if everything's going to be different, if everything's going to be filled with possibility and opportunity, how will I know if I'm ready? How will I know how to deal?

And it's not like Zoë ever worried about these things. "Better to ask forgiveness than permission," she'd say. And God knows she doled out her fair share of apologies. But still, nothing ever fazed her. Nothing ever tripped her up. She just moved through life at lightning speed, expecting nothing but cooperation, approval, laughter, and fun.

Zoë was street smart and naïve.

She was thoughtful yet reckless.

She was sexy but innocent.

She was a walking dichotomy.

And I want to be just like her.

I climb out of bed, grab my backpack, and retrieve the cobalt blue book that Marc gave me. Then I switch on my reading light, slip back between the sheets, and with totally shaking hands, turn to the first page, shivering when I see her familiar, round, loopy scrawl, and read:

This is Zoë's diary. And you should NOT be reading it!

I knew she was right. But I also knew she had something to teach me. So I ignored the warning, and turned the page.

Nine

June 14 (finally!)

I don't know why they call it the last day of school, when really it's the first day of freedom. Cuz the second that minimum day bell rings at 12:20 P.M., there's not a teacher, principal, or school administrator w/in 50 miles that can touch me—and that includes YOU, Coach Warner, you disgusting old pig. You think I don't notice when you look down my top? Next year I'm gonna stick a tiny mirror down there so you can see your own ugly reflection staring back at you!!!

As usual, classes were a joke—everyone just ignoring the teachers, running around, signing yearbooks, and promising to hook up sometime during the hot days ahead. All I could do was nod and smile and go through the motions, because the whole entire time I was thinking about ditching Stephen so I can hook up with Marc.

I know he's into me.
I'm never wrong about these things.

June 15

Didn't make it downstairs 'til after 11, still feeling drunk from last night. Walked right into the edge of the kitchen table and had to grab the corner to steady myself. Thank G nobody noticed. Dad had his nose buried in a pile of papers (as usual), Mom was outside working in her overachiever garden wearing her big old hat, SPF 75, wrap-around sunglasses, gloves, and a long-sleeved shirt—like she's allergic to the sun or something. Only Echo sniffed the air as I passed, flashed me a knowing look, but didn't say a word as I headed for the coffeemaker. Didn't even get to the second sip before Carly called, wanting to bitch me out for ditching Stephen and trying to hook up with Marc behind his back.

So I reminded her that I'm her BFF, NOT Stephen. I'm the one who covered for her that time when she said she was at my house but was really out with H, not to mention the gazillion other favors I've done for her over the last 5 years. Not to mention that Marc was already gone by the time I finally made it outside, so no damage done, right?

But even after I reminded her of all that she still has the nerve to go, "Yeah, but still."

I mean, I love Carly, really I do. But this holier than thou crap has got to stop.

Maybe she should get together with Stephen if she cares so much about his stupid feelings.

June 16

I'm psychic! Just call me Claire Voyant. Because the very last line I wrote in my very last entry came true. That's right, Carly hooked up with Stephen. And I'm not even that mad about it. Really. I barely even care. Well, other than the fact that she went behind my back. But really, as far as I'm concerned she can have him because I am sooooo over him. I'm sick of how his life revolves around sports and those stupid instant replays he insists on watching over and over and over again. I'm sick of the way he eats with his mouth open, all those chucked up particles tossing from side to side as he laughs out loud at his own lame-ass jokes. But mostly I'm sick of the way he bicep peeks during sex. It's like he gets more excited watching the way they bulge out than by seeing me naked beneath him. And if I sound like some bitter old hausfrau who got married too young, and stayed married too long, well, then, whose fault is that? He stole a year of my life, robbed me of time I'll never get back.

Not to mention how it's been totally obvious from the start how Carly's been crushing on him, since day one. It's like she's been waiting this entire time for me to dump him. Even the six months she was with H, she was just passing time. So if she wants him that bad, she can have him. I hope they're very happy together, really I do.

I just think she could've waited 'til I'd actually broken up with him first. I just think she could've waited 'til things were official. Not to mention how she could have at least pretended to look guilty when I walked in on them.

But instead she just looked up and said, "Well you said you were gonna leave him."

Which, of course, made Stephen gawk at me in shock. But I just kept right on looking at her. Shaking my head as I used her words right back at her, saying, "Yeah, but still."

Then I went back downstairs and ended up smoking some really powerful shit with Kevin and Kristin who are so freaking in love they'll probably get married or something. I mean it's just so weird how they've been together *since eighth grade, and how they never ever think about what they could be missing.*

I'm always thinking about what I'm missing.

Even when I'm happy with what I have.

Anyway, we just hung in the backyard, looking at the stars 'til we were cold and hungry and misted with dew. And everything felt so vast, and unlimited, and extremely close to perfect.

But now I have to figure out a way to fill up the summer before my parents decide that for me. So, good luck to me!

I stifle a yawn, and close Zoë's diary, sliding it under my mattress for safekeeping. Not one thing I read surprised me. Seriously, not the drugs, not the sex, not even that whole big drama with Carly. Though I'd always been kind of curious why she stopped coming over so much. I guess I just assumed it had something to do with Marc. But then Zoë's life had always been dramatic, and mysterious, and far more adventurous than mine. And even though I like Carly, I know it had to be a pretty tough gig to be my sister's best friend. I mean, Zoë was just one of those people who the clouds always cleared for, the sun always shined on, and the stars came out for.

She's the reason they invented spotlights.

And she left anyone standing next to her feeling like a dull, spent bulb.

But what did surprise me was the way I felt as I was reading. So close to Zoë, like she was sitting right there beside me, whispering the words in my ear, and urging me to turn the page.

And it feels so good to finally have her back, that I switch off the light and close my eyes, saving Zoë for another day.

Ten

By Monday at school Jenay and Chess are officially a couple. Though that's really no surprise for those of us forced to watch them make out for the remainder of my party. And as I head for the lunch table that has gotten so crowded we've merged with the one beside it, I actually have to fight the urge to just turn around and bolt.

I mean, where would I go? Back to junior high? Because obviously, that's no longer an option. So instead I take a deep breath and smile at everyone, including Parker—who I've managed to avoid until now.

"Hey," I say, dropping my lunch on the table, and easing onto the long yellow bench.

Jenay smiles then goes right back to her story, and by the time she's finished everyone is laughing. Well, everyone but me. Since it's the one about how when she and Abby were watching her baby brother and he squirted them both in the face just as they were changing his diaper, which believe me, I've heard like a million times before.

So I just reach into my lunch pack and retrieve my sandwich, trying to ignore the fact that Parker is waving at me, trying to get my attention.

"Hey, wake up," he says, leaning toward me and smiling. "I called you last night but it went straight to voice mail. I got your number from Jenay. I hope that's okay?"

"Oh, sorry about that," I say, twisting the top off my Snapple and taking a sip. "My phone was off, and by the time I realized you'd called . . ." I just shrug, letting that trail off to nothing. Because the truth is, it's not like I was going to call him back anyway. And it's not because I don't like him, I mean, I'm not exactly sure how I feel about him. It's mostly because I'm so freaking lame I don't know what to say after "hello."

"Did you have a good weekend?" he asks.

I think about the book I read, the homework I finished, Zoë's diary, and shrug. "Yeah. You?"

He nods, still leaning toward me, still smiling, still gazing at me with those deep blue eyes.

But when I see him looking at me like that, ignoring everyone else just so he can concentrate solely on me, it makes me feel so freaked out, so nervous, and so totally inadequate, that I stand up and say, "Um, I'll be right back."

Then I abandon my lunch, abandon the table, and run out the door, desperate for fresh air and a temporary respite from the worst part of me—the pathetic, fearful, morbidly insecure part. The part that wonders why a guy as cute as Parker would ever like a girl as dorky as me, why anyone anywhere would ever like me.

I run past the burnout tree, the one where all the hard-core partiers hang, thinking how they're the only group in this whole entire school who never point, stare, or whisper as I pass.

But maybe that's because they're just too stoned to care. I mean the cheerleaders, the song leaders, the drill teamers, the mascots, the jocks, the drama freaks, the band geeks, the science nerds, the fashionistas, the club leaders, the council reps, the Goths, the Preps, the ROTC marchers, the girls who starve to be skinny, the girls who barf to be skinny, the scrawny guys, the wannabes, the techies, the sluts, the virgins, the cutters, the Future Farmers of America, the alterna artists, the rainbow kids—the one thing they all have in common is that they all stare at me. Every single one of them. But the major druggies? Not so much. So it feels pretty safe to pass by.

I head toward the bathroom, even though I don't really plan on going inside. But it's good to have as a decoy route in case Abby decides to come looking for me again. And then just as I turn down the hall where I'd planned to lean against the wall until the bell rings, I see Marc sitting not two feet away.

"Oh. Hey," I say, surprised to not only run into him again, but also to see that he's smoking, on campus, as though it's actually allowed or something.

He just looks at me and nods, squinting his eyes as he takes another drag.

"I was just on my way to—" I point straight ahead, feeling the need to explain my presence, yet feeling embarrassed by how fake I sound.

But he just drops his cigarette, smashes it with his thick, rubber-soled boot, looks up at me, and goes, "Did you read it?"

I gaze down at the ground, not wanting him to know.

Then he gets up from the bench and brushes right past me. "You will when you're ready," he says, walking away.

"Where the heck did you go? Parker thinks you hate him." Jenay merges her brows together and shakes her head. "He waited so long, he was late to class."

"Why would I hate him?" I ask, focusing my guilt-ridden gaze on the sidewalk, as we head toward home.

"Uh, because you ran off and never returned? I'm serious, Echo, you should've seen him. He just sat there with your lunch right in front of him, wondering if he should save it, eat it, toss it, or what."

She's staring at me, I can feel it. But since Abby's in the middle, that means I'll have to go through her if I want to confirm it. And I feel really uncomfortable talking about all of this, partly because it makes me feel weird, inept, and embarrassed, but also because I know Abby likes Parker too. She has for years. She just won't admit it.

But Abby's totally on to me, and she's not about to let me off easy. "Don't be going all AWOL on my account. So what if I think he's cute. I think a lot of guys are cute. And it's not like I was all attached or anything," she says, kicking a rock out of her path and shrugging like she really doesn't care. "So if you really like him, then just go for it, Echo. Don't hold back because of me."

"*Do* you like him?" Jenay asks, her eyes growing hopeful and wide as she waits for a definite answer.

Only the thing is, I don't have a definite answer. Because I'm not really sure how I feel. Though I do know there's a "right" answer, one that will make her happy, and hopefully put an end to all of this. So I take a deep breath and say, "Totally. I mean, why wouldn't I? He's cute, and sweet, and smart. And it's not like there's anything wrong with him, right?"

The second that's out, Abby starts cracking up. I mean full body bent over laughing, while Jenay just rolls her eyes and shakes her head and goes, "That's it? You like him because there's nothing *wrong* with him? You like him because he has no *obvious defects*? Jeez Echo, that's real romantic stuff. I mean, you're just head over heels then, aren't you?"

"No, I just . . ." I gaze back down at the ground, wondering who I'm trying to convince more, me or her. "I like him," I finally say. "Okay? Happy now? He's really nice, and a really good kisser too." I peek at both of them, feeling relieved when I see Jenay smile, hoping that means she believes me.

"Then it's settled. He can ask you to homecoming and you won't say no?" Jenay asks, her voice full of hope. "Cause it would be really fun if we could double date, don't you think?"

I nod at Jenay and then gaze at Abby. But she's no longer looking at me. She's busy staring straight ahead.

Eleven

Two days before the dance, I tell my mom I need a dress. Though of course Jenay had already bought hers, like the day after my party. And Parker, just naturally assuming I'd already gotten mine too, kept quizzing me about the color so his mom could order a matching corsage.

I didn't have the heart to tell him that I hadn't bothered to even think about a dress, much less go look for one. So I lied and said I was torn between a black one and a white one, so any old flowers should do.

"It would've been nice if you could've given me just a little more notice," my mom says, shaking her head as she trolls through the racks, trying to find something pretty and affordable that won't make me look like a slut.

I just stand there, amazed by the show of emotion. It's been so long since she's expressed sadness, annoyance, or anything stronger than zombie-like calm.

"Zoë and I always used to make a day of it. We'd buy the dress, have lunch, and then go looking for a bag, jewelry, and shoes. But this, this two days' notice." She shakes her head again, this time pursing her lips. "What if we need alterations? Did you ever consider that?" She looks at me, eyes clearly alarmed at the thought. Well, as alarmed as those happy pills allow.

But I just shrug. I mean, even though it's nice to see her thawing out of her usual, icy numbness, I really don't appreciate having to compete with Zoë. Especially when I'm so clearly the loser. I mean, I may be the good, obedient, straight-A daughter, but Zoë was the exciting one. Zoë was the fun one. Zoë was the glamorous one. Zoë was the kind of daughter you actually miss.

"Well, I guess if it's too long, I'll just get higher heels or something," I finally say, determined to ignore that last slight of hers and get through the rest of the day unscathed.

But she just ignores that, presses a handful of dresses into my arms, and goes, "Here. It's a start. Now where the heck is that salesgirl?"

If you were going to categorize my mom, you'd obviously choose words like "organized," "controlling," and "type-A personality." But that doesn't mean she can't be relaxed, compassionate, or fun. Though in the last year, it's like she's been riding an emotional roller coaster, and it's been kind of hard to adjust to all of the surprising twists and turns.

I mean, everything started off all fine and well. One of her papers finally got published and she was actually awarded tenure, which is like a really big deal. But then the whole Zoë thing happened, and she headed straight into this rapid descent, her tears and depression building at an alarming speed until one day, after an extended couch-sitting, food-avoiding, sleep-depriving crying jag, she reached for that bottle of doctor-prescribed happy pills, and ever since it's been miles of flat track, allowing for a safe but boring ride.

But that little show of annoyance back there in the store, when she compared me to Zoë and got all upset? Well, that's something she's never actually done before. And I wonder if it signals another drop ahead, one that I won't realize until it's too late.

"Well, under the conditions, I'd say that went much better than I anticipated," she says, carefully placing her linen napkin across the lap of her jeans, but not those high-rise, tapered-ankle, multipleated "mom jeans" (thank God), but still, dark blue and no-nonsense. "And you've got quite the figure, young lady. Who knew?" She raises her thin, arched eyebrows and cracks a brief smile.

"Yeah, quite the stick figure," I say, gazing down at my nearly concave chest, wondering if it will ever progress.

"Don't kid yourself. You've got your great-aunt Eleanor's figure." She nods, her short, brown, wash-and-wear hair barely moving. "And she was a model for Saks."

I think about Zoë, and how she always wanted to be a model, and I wonder if my mom ever said that to her.

"So tell me about this young man." She leans forward, taking a sip of iced tea.

I gaze down at my lap, knowing she's only trying to connect, and wishing I felt more comfortable talking about things like this. "Well, I've known him forever, but we never really hung out until now, and I don't know, his best friend asked Jenay, and so, he asked me." I shrug, using my straw to move the lemon wedge and block of ice that's impeding my progress to the good stuff below.

"Do you like him?" she asks, as though we always engage in these heart-to-heart girl talks, as though nothing's changed, like we're just picking up right where we left off. And it's been so long since she even tried, that it makes me want to give the right answer, the one that will keep it going, the one that will keep her feeling this way.

But I also don't want to lie. So instead, I just nod.

"Well, your father and I are looking forward to meeting him. And I'm so glad we went with that cobalt blue dress, aren't you? I was thinking maybe a silver purse and shoes? What are your thoughts?"

I reach for my menu and pretend to read it. "Um, I guess something cute and dressy, that I can actually walk in without falling over." I shrug.

"I know just the place." She nods.

The whole time Jenay's stepmom is taking our picture, all I can think about is Abby. And how she's missing. And how she should be standing right here beside us, overdressed, overexcited, and anxious to take part in her first limo, first dance, and first date too. But even though Jenay tried her best to set her up, Abby wouldn't have anything to do with it. Insisting she had a "family thing" that'd been planned for months, and that she'd "completely forgotten all about."

But I know better. I know Abby's just romantic enough to want a date who asked her for real, and stubborn enough to insist on that, or not go at all.

"Okay, everyone, just lean in, a little bit closer. Echo, move your hair out of your eyes so I can see your beautiful face," Jenay's stepmom says, the fingers on her free hand directing us toward the center, while she holds the tiny digital camera with the other. "Perfect. Hold it . . . great. One more. Okay, I'll e-mail copies to all of your parents." She leans against Jenay's dad and smiles. "Oops! There goes Landon! I knew it wouldn't last. Okay, have fun everyone, and girls, you look gorgeous!"

She hugs Jenay and me, careful not to mess up our hair,

then runs upstairs to the nursery in her bare feet, snug jeans, and tight pink T-shirt, with her stream of blond hair trailing behind her, making her look more like Jenay's hip older sister than her father's second wife.

"Okay, the limo's outside waiting. So everyone, be good, have fun, and stay out of trouble," her dad says, delivering the exact same speech my dad gave, just half an hour before.

One by one we crawl into the back of the limo, sliding across the long, leather seat. The second the door is closed and the driver pulls away from the curb, Jenay leans her head back, heaves a dramatic sigh, and goes, "Thank God that's over."

Chess grabs her hand and smiles. "What do you mean? Your mom's really nice, and your dad seems cool too." He shrugs.

"Well, she's actually my stepmom. My real mom died when I was little, and my dad didn't remarry until about four years ago. So yeah, she's nice and all, and it's good to have a mom again and not be the only girl in the house for a change. But still, parents, you know?" She smiles.

"Echo's parents are way cool," Parker says, obviously wanting to say something positive, even if it means he has to lie.

But Jenay and I just look at each other and burst out laughing. And even though it's really not all that funny, every time we look at each other we laugh that much harder. And I know it's kind of rude, and I know it excludes the guys, but still, being able to share a private joke like this makes me feel calmer, reminding me how whatever happens tonight, we're both in it together.

We go to this restaurant called the Blue Water Grill even though our town is completely landlocked and there's no blue water anywhere to be found (including the lake at the park where the water is polluted, murky, and brown). I mean, let's face it, a name like that can't help but conjure up images of vast ocean views and glamorous diners docking their yachts, before strolling inside for a nice sunset meal.

But here, instead of ocean views, you get a parking lot. And instead of a yacht, you get a smiling, plywood, cartoon pelican ushering you into the nautical-themed interior that's a lot closer to Moby Dick than luxury liner.

The hostess leads us to a table where Teresa and Sean, Lisa and Drew, and Kaitlin and Mike are already waiting, and I spend the entire time fiddling with my menu and napkin and pretty much doing whatever it takes to keep my hands busy and as far away from Parker's as possible.

I know I'm acting all weird and uptight and ridiculous, and it's not like I can even explain why. I mean, I used to love watching Zoë get ready for all her school dances, and I could hardly wait for the day when it would be my turn. I even used to dream about us going together, you know double-dating, just two cool sisters and their cute, hottie boyfriends, sharing a limo and acting all glamorous and sophisticated. And even after I learned how Zoë and her friends usually only stayed long enough to take the formal pictures before heading out to go party somewhere else, that still didn't change it for me.

I guess it just always seemed like Zoë was part of this mysterious, grown-up world, one that I couldn't wait to join. Only now that I'm being admitted, I no longer feel ready. And since everything Zoë did was always bigger, and brighter, and better than everyone else, I know that no matter how hard I try, I'll never be able to match her.

"Did I tell you how much I love your dress? That color is like, *so* amazing," Teresa says, leaning close to the bathroom mirror and applying a layer of pale pink lip gloss over the dark pink lipstick she just applied.

I gaze down the length of my dress, all the way to my

strappy sandals, amazed at how it all came together so much better than I ever would've guessed.

"You and Parker are so cute together," she says, dropping her lip gloss into her bag and moving on to her blond high-lighted hair, which has been professionally twisted, curled, and pinned into the world's most complicated updo.

I force my face into a smile, watching as she fishes around in her green, oversized tote bag, which I have to admit looks incredibly odd with her pink shiny dress and gold shoes.

"Want some?" she asks, retrieving a water bottle filled with some kind of red homemade brew. "I brought enough for everyone. That's why this bag is so big, in case you were won-dering." She laughs. "I'll probably pass them out in the limos. But let's just get a head start and take a little hit now, K?" She unscrews the lid and takes a long, hearty sip. Then she shoves it toward me, urging me on with her wide, blue eyes. "Go ahead." She nods. "It's awesome. So sweet you can barely taste the alcohol."

I hesitate, but only for a moment. Then I tilt the bottle back and take a gulp. A much bigger gulp than I'd planned. Then I close my eyes and realize she's right. It is sweet. And other than the sting, burning its way down my throat, I can hardly taste the vodka.

Twelve

The second the band starts playing a slow song, I try to bolt for the bathroom. But then Parker grabs my arm and says, "No way. Forget it. Step away from the vodka, and come with me."

I grip his hand tightly as I follow behind, hoping he'll understand that my sudden display of hand passion has more to do with the effects of drinking than any romantic or passionate connection, because if I've bonded with anyone tonight it would definitely be Teresa, the former Queen Bee of Parkview Junior High. The girl with the moonshine water bottles.

I mean Jenay, now free to make out with Chess whenever she chooses and no longer needing alcohol as an excuse, took only a sip or two, before giving her bottle away. And even though everyone else was pretty much drinking on the way to the dance, it was Teresa and I who kept at it long after we'd arrived. And it's not that I actually like it all that much, because to be honest, it really is a little too sweet. But with Jenay totally focused on Chess and ignoring me, there's no way I can *not* drink and still manage to have a good time.

It's like, I've barely finished my bottle, and already I'm feeling lighter, looser, and free. More like my sister, and a lot less like me.

"Are you having fun?" Parker asks, tightening his grip on my waist and pulling me closer.

"Um, yeah." I shrug, gazing around at all the sparkly silver decorations, the fake snow at the edge of the stage, and the hot, sweaty lead singer, his eyes shut tight as he wails into the microphone, singing a song about lost love.

At first it all seems so pretty and sparkly, but soon it turns blurry and bendy. And when Parker brings his hand to my cheek and says, "Look at me," I push him away and rush for the door, mumbling something about needing some air.

"Are you okay?" he asks, concern in his voice as he trails close behind.

I rock from foot to foot, hugging myself with both arms, not having considered the cold in my rush to be free. All I wanted was some time alone, so I could clear my head, settle my stomach, and stand in the dark, watching my breath escape my body and then disappear into the night.

What I didn't want was for Parker to tag along. Partly because I wasn't sure if I was going to be sick, and partly because I'm not sure I'm ready for Parker, and me, and all that we entail. But now that he's here, I don't want him to think I'm a freak. So I try to say something just to fill up the quiet.

"Which one do you think is ours?" I ask, motioning to the long line of black shiny limos, as Parker removes his jacket and places it over my narrow, pale, goose bump–covered shoulders.

He squints across the parking lot and smiles. "Third one," he says, nodding like he's sure.

"No way." I shake my head and gaze at the long line of generic cars. "I mean, how can you even tell? They all look alike."

"See the guy standing next to it? He's our driver." He nods. "I can tell by the hat."

"They all wear hats, its part of the uniform," I say, gazing at him and laughing in spite of myself.

"Trust me. I can tell. His hat is different." He looks at me, those gorgeous blue eyes that used to ignore me, now searching for mine.

And even though my head has cleared, my stomach still feels a little weird. But I know it's just nerves. I also know how to get through it. "Wanna bet?" I ask, suddenly feeling better, braver, using Zoë as my guide.

"Bet what?" He gives me a dubious yet interested look.

"That you're wrong. That you're totally, completely off base. Because there's no way you can tell from all the way over here if that guy's really our driver." I look him in the eye, my gaze steady and sure, my mouth curving into a smile.

"And if I'm right?" he asks, obviously interested in where this might lead.

"Then you win." I shrug.

"Yeah, but *what* do I win?" He smiles as he moves in closer, quickly adapting to the new me. "It's a bet. So there's got to be a prize, right?"

I look at him, gazing directly into his eyes for the first time tonight. "Oh, there's a prize all right. But you won't know what it is until it's too late and you've already lost." I laugh, grabbing hold of his hand and pulling him across the lot, all the way over to limo number three.

"Hey," Parker says, reaching out to slap hands with the chauffeur, who squeezes his cell phone between his shoulder and ear so he can slap back.

"You guys ready to leave?" He places his hand over the mouthpiece, and gazes from Parker to me.

"No, we're just—" Parker starts, but I cut him off.

"I just need to get something out of the back. It'll only take a sec." I smile, watching as he winks at Parker before walking away.

"So, about this prize," Parker says, closing the door and appearing by my side so fast and seamless it's like he has springs in his shoes, ones that activate at the first hint of sex.

I look into his eyes and wait, knowing that soon, he'll lean in to kiss me.

We kiss for a while. And while it's nice, and sweet, and way better than that time in the closet since there's no bad smells or hockey sticks shoved against my butt, I'm still not fully convinced that he actually wants to make out with me—boring, inept, plain Jane me.

So in my head, I imagine I'm Zoë—that I'm beautiful, wild, glamorous, and experienced—that there's nothing in the world that can scare me.

And as Parker wraps his arms around my waist, I slide my hands down the front of his shirt, making my way down to his pants, hesitating near the spot that I would never try to touch, but that Zoë wouldn't think twice about.

"I don't get you," he whispers, suddenly pulling away. "It's like, inside the dance you'd barely even look at me, but now?" He shakes his head and squints, obviously not complaining, but still, more than a little perplexed.

But I just smile, knowing I'm no longer me. I ditched that nervous loser and became someone better. "I lost the bet," I say, gazing at him with Zoë's eyes, touching him with Zoë's hands, and kissing him with Zoë's lips.

He kisses me on the neck, as I lean back against the seat, feeling so incredibly daring and free. Then he slips his finger under my blue silk strap, sliding it all the way down, as I turn my head and gaze toward the window, shocked to see my own dull reflection staring back at me.

"I can't do this," I say, pushing him away, frantically reaching for my strap.

Parker just looks at me, his face flushed and confused, his hands halted in panic. "But you seemed so—"

I turn back toward the window, hoping not to see me, feeling disappointed when I do.

"Echo, really, I didn't mean . . . please don't be mad," he says, his hands fumbling awkwardly as he reaches for me, trying to make me face him.

I move farther away, my heart beating frantically as I run my hands through my hair and over my dress, erasing all evidence of my little digression, knowing I need to act fast, to come up with some excuse that will explain my bizarre behavior, so everything will get back to normal and stop being so weird. "Jeez Parker, it was only a limo bet. I mean, just how big a prize did you think you were gonna get?" I ask, chasing it with a laugh so he'll think we're okay.

He laughs too, his eyes relaxing, his face clearly relieved. Then he opens the door and steps onto the curb, offering his hand as a guide. "Well, I probably should've told you this before, and I hope you're not too mad, but I have a confession to make," he says, slipping his arm through mine as we head back inside.

I gaze up at him, happy that we've moved on, but only mildly interested in what it might be.

"That wasn't really our limo." He smiles.

Thirteen

The next morning when I woke I didn't feel nearly as bad as I expected. Or at least not in a physical way. I mean, I didn't throw up, I didn't have a headache, and I didn't feel the slightest bit queasy. Which basically means that all of my parents' warnings about the "high price one always pays for a night of overindulgence," didn't come true for me.

But mentally? Mentally I felt like crap. And I don't remember anyone ever cautioning me about that.

I roll over and gaze out the window, noticing how the big oak tree has lost most of its leaves, making it look stark, alone, and defensive. Or maybe that's just me. Maybe I'm getting all Freudian and weird, projecting all of my innermost feelings onto a tree. I mean after last night, and that whole freaky limo episode, I found myself feeling pretty stark, alone, and defensive too.

Yet I was also aware of how I was quite possibly making a

snowstorm out of a snowflake. I mean, there are tons of girls who practically line up to "go wild" and who end up going a whole lot further than that. And it's not like you ever see any of them stopping to think twice, or mentally torturing themselves like me.

But clearly, I'm nothing like those girls. And I'm obviously nothing like Zoë. And even though I know my life would be way more fun if I was, the truth is, I have no idea how to act like that and not lose myself in the process.

"I can't believe you actually brought your books," Teresa says, eyeing my bulging backpack and laughing.

"You said we were gonna study," I say, cringing at how whiny I sound, while wondering what I missed. I mean, earlier, when we were on the phone, I specifically heard her use the word "study." So excuse me for taking that literally.

"Well, I also said we were going to the library, but you don't see me heading there now, do you? The only reason I said all that is 'cause my mom has ginormous elephant ears, and she was totally listening to our conversation that whole time."

"So where are we going?" I ask, walking alongside her, my way-too-heavy backpack digging a wedge deep into my shoulder.

"The park. I told some people we'd meet them."

"What people?" I look at her, noticing for the first time how she's dressed so differently from how I'm used to seeing her at school, way less preppy and a lot more sexy.

"Just some guys, no one you know." She smiles.

"Like, friends of Sean's?" I ask, wondering why she's acting so undercover and secretive.

But she just laughs. "Please. Sean is totally sweet, don't get me wrong, and he's good for school dances and stuff like that, but, well, I don't know. There's this other guy, and it's kind of hard to explain." She shrugs. "But you'll see what I mean when you meet him."

When we get to the park, instead of going right down to the lake like I usually do, Teresa leads me over to the old fountain, the one with all the angels and cherubs and overblown biblical images, all molded from a single slab of cement.

"Omigod! There he is, Jason. He is *so* hot! So just act cool, okay?" she whispers, shooting me a doubtful look, obviously not convinced I'll be able to pull it off. She fluffs her hair around her shoulders, then straightens her sweater and picks up the pace, heading straight for these two guys who are drinking, smoking, and just overall loitering on the fountain's tiled edge.

"Hey," she says, stopping before them and tilting her head toward me. "This is Echo."

I gaze at the two of them, wondering which one of these delinquents she could possibly think is hot.

"Echo? Who names their kid that? What're your parents, like, hippies?" This comes from a fat guy wearing a size too small I DO MY OWN NUDE SCENES T-shirt that I hope is meant to be ironic. And when he laughs his whole belly shakes, stretching and bulging against the overburdened cotton, just like jolly ol' St. Nick. Only a whole lot grosser.

I stand there, wondering how soon I can leave, when Teresa shakes her head, pushes him playfully on the shoulder, and says, "Tom, you asshole. Leave her alone. Echo's cool." But when she looks at me, her expression tells a whole other story, having already decided I'm not.

She pulls a pack of cigarettes from her purse and settles herself onto the ground, sitting Indian style at their feet. "Somebody give me a light," she says, offering the pack to me, as the other guy, the one I'm assuming is "Hot Jason," leans toward her with a burning match.

I shake my head as I watch her inhale, then release it back

through her nose and mouth like an angry cartoon bull. Making sure to shift just ever so slightly, so that the V of her low-cut sweater is aimed straight at Jason—who's aiming for slick but nailing seedy, and who's definitely old enough to know better.

It's weird how she acts like this around me, yet plays it so straight at school. Like last night, when she was drinking, only I saw how much. And I'm willing to bet I'm the only one who knows about the smoking, the cleavage flaunting, and how she's hoping to cheat on Sean with this loser.

"How's your little boyfriend? What's his name? Sam?" asks Tom, who's already been called an asshole, and now seems intent on proving it.

"His name is Sean, you moron. And he's not my boyfriend, we just hang sometimes." She glances quickly at Jason, with his slicked-back, longish blond hair, faded Levis, motorcycle boots, dark T-shirt, and black leather jacket. And I realize he seems really familiar, though I can't imagine why.

"You go there too?" Tom asks, kicking his foot in my general direction, as opposed to, oh, I don't know, gesturing politely or addressing me by name.

"Bella Vista? Um, yeah," I say, feeling pretty squeamish under his heavy, judgmental gaze, and wondering not for the first time, why I'm still here.

"That school sucks. Principal Hames is a fucking loser! L-O-S-E-R," he says, pumping his beer-gripping fist in the air, proving he can spell.

I just stand there, not agreeing, not denying, not saying a word. Just trying to avoid the secondhand smoke while plotting my escape.

"You leaving soon?" he asks, dragging on his cigarette and sipping his beer, going from beer to cigarette, from cigarette to beer, barely taking a break in between.

"Bella Vista? No, I just started," I say, looking at Teresa who's ignoring me now, since she's too busy flirting with Jason.

"No, I mean now. You're just standing there like you've got an appointment or something." He sips his beer and laughs. "At least drop your bag and relax. It's not like we're gonna hurt you. Unless you want us to." He narrows his eyes, giving me a long, leisurely once-over, starting at my Converse tennis shoes and working his way to the top of my head.

"Oh, no, I just . . ." I gaze at Teresa who's still ignoring me, then I turn back toward the way we came. I mean, not to be a prude, but I don't like this scene. And not to be a freak, but I'm getting a really bad vibe.

"You guys got any more beer?" Teresa asks, getting the attention back on her, which believe me, is where we both want it. "I need a little hair of the dog. I swear I have like the worst hangover, *ever*. Echo and I got totally wasted last night, and I need some relief." She stands, moving toward Jason and grabbing his beer, tilting her head back and swinging her long blond hair as she guzzles.

"Want some?" she says, turning to me, her eyes wide and shiny, her mouth wet and open.

But I just shake my head and look away, cringing as my overloaded backpack carves a long, deep groove into the top of my shoulder.

"Your friend's a real blast," Tom says, tossing his bottle toward the silver metal trash can, not bothering to get up and retrieve it when it ricochets off the side and rolls across the grass.

Then just as I'm about to tell him to go pound sand (or something much worse), Jason flicks his lit cigarette right at him and goes, "Shut the fuck up." Then his eyes move over to me, embarking on an unhurried cruise along my skinny, undeveloped body, until finally coming to rest upon mine. "I knew your sister," he says, reaching for another beer, flipping the top, and nodding. Smiling as he pulls Teresa close, pressing her hard against him, and sliding his hand down her back until he reaches her butt and squeezes. His eyes never once wavering from mine.

I watch as Teresa gazes up at him and giggles, then I turn and walk away. Feeling angry with her for dragging me here, but even angrier with myself for staying.

"Echo, wait! Shit. You guys, I'll be right back," Teresa says, running to catch up with me. "Where the hell are you going?" she whispers, tugging on my jacket, as I pick up the pace, doing my best to ignore her. "Echo, jeez, don't be mad."

I shake my head and walk even faster, 'til I'm just short of running. I hate when people do that. I hate when they put you in a really bad position and then tell you how you should feel about it.

"Seriously, slow down, please? Just give me a sec to explain," she pleads.

I swing around and face her, making no attempt to hide my anger.

"Listen, I know Tom's kind of an asshole, and I probably should've warned you. I'm sorry, okay?"

"*Kind of* an asshole?" I look at her and shake my head. "Oh my God, you weren't trying to set me up with him, were you?" My eyes go wide, having just now thought of that totally disgusting possibility.

But she just rolls her eyes and shakes her head. "Don't be ridiculous. I know you're all into Parker, and I would never try to mess with that. It's just that I really, really, really like Jason. I mean I *really* like him. Don't you think he's cute?" she asks, moving right past me and back to her. Going from apology to confession in zero to five seconds.

"Honestly? I think he's creepy. Not to mention *old*," I say, far too mad to even care what she thinks.

"But that's why I like him." She shrugs. "He's got a car,

money, and ten times the maturity of all the guys at school put together."

"Teresa, he's a *drug dealer*," I say, not entirely sure of this, but still convinced that it's true. "He's bad news. Trust me, you *don't* want to get involved with him."

But she just sucks on her cigarette and squints at me, and it's clear she's chosen not to listen. "You don't even know him. You just met him like, ten minutes ago."

I watch as she shakes her head and rolls her eyes, even though everything she just said is wrong. I mean, even though I haven't actually "met" him until now, that doesn't mean I don't know *about* him. But it's not like I'm gonna explain that to her, since it's not like she'd even listen if I tried. The only thing I want to do is just get the heck out of here. Now.

"Listen," I finally say. "You're right. It probably is none of my business. But maybe you should ask yourself why some twenty-five-year-old guy is hanging out with and supplying beer and drugs to a fifteen-year-old girl. I mean, come *on,* Teresa." But when I look at her, her eyes are blazing. And instead of persuading her, I've just made her mad.

"Okay, first of all, he's twenty-four, *not* twenty-five. And second, you only saw him give me a light and a beer. *That's all*. So you better not go telling people anything other than that. In fact, you better not go telling them anything at all. You also shouldn't be so judgmental. I mean, he was friends with your sister."

I look at her, standing before me, feeling so righteous even though she couldn't be more wrong. "He *knew* my sister, but he was *never* her friend," I say, glaring at her. "Believe me, there's a difference."

But she just rolls her eyes and flicks her ash to the ground, the gray and black particles hovering briefly before clinging to her feet. "Listen," she says, grabbing my arm just as I start to walk away. "No need to mention any of this at school, okay? I

mean, it's not like it's anybody's business, and I don't want
Sean to get all upset and get the wrong idea. All right?" She
looks at me, her face showing fear for the first time today.

But I just release myself from her grip and head toward
home. "Don't worry," I say without looking back. "I won't say
a word."

Fourteen

Monday at lunch Teresa's sitting next to Sean, acting all cuddly and cute, like yesterday never happened. I line up my food, spreading it out before me, gazing from my orange to my cookie to my sandwich, wondering which to eat first.

"I can't believe your mom still packs a lunch for you," Teresa says, eyeballing my pastrami on rye. "I think that is *so* sweet."

I decide to skip the healthy stuff and just start with the chocolate chip cookie, wondering if by "sweet" what she really means is "juvenile."

"My mom would never take the time to do that," she continues, popping a tiny powdered donut into her mouth before washing it down with a slug of Diet Coke.

I chew my cookie, trying to think of a good response. *I'm the baby so she likes to take care of me? No, too babyish. I'm all she has left? Jeez, way too morbid.* So finally I just say, "Yeah, well, that's just her." But then I remember how that was never really her, at least not until the happy pills moved in.

"Hey, what happened yesterday? Your cell was off, and your mom said you were out," Parker says, kissing the top of my head and squeezing in beside me.

"Oh, yeah, I—" I start to give an excuse, but then Teresa butts in, deciding to provide one for me.

"I needed a little help with my homework, and Echo totally saved my life. Did you know she's like a mathematical genius?" She gives me a quick warning glance, one that nobody notices but me, then she smiles and rubs her shoulder lightly against Sean's.

"Wow, cute, nice, and good at math too?" Parker says, winking as he steals the rest of my cookie.

I just gaze at Teresa and shrug. "So she says."

After school I meet Abby at her locker. Only this time, Jenay's not there.

"She had a pep club meeting," Abby says, slamming her locker a little harder than necessary and looking at me. "I mean, *pep club*! Can you even believe it?"

I shrug my shoulders and walk beside her as we make our way off campus. "So how was your weekend, you know, the whole family thing?" I ask, not wanting to talk about Jenay behind her back, yet feeling like I have to at least keep up the appearance of believing Abby's excuse for not going to the dance.

But she just peers at me from the corner of her eye and sighs. "Okay, I think we both know there was no family thing," she says, shaking her head and looking away. "So go ahead, tell me everything. Was it awesome?"

"It was okay," I say, nervously shifting my backpack, not

wanting to make her feel any worse by yammering on and on about it.

"Just okay?" She raises her eyebrows and waits.

"Yeah, I mean, it was fun." I nod, wishing we could move away from this subject too.

"Well, I gotta tell ya, Jenay makes it sound a lot more exciting than you. I mean, you did go to the same dance, right?" She laughs.

"Even shared a limo." I shrug.

"Well, you should hear her version. She dropped by yesterday, and went on and on and on. By the time she left, I felt like *I* was the one dating Chess. Seriously, I'm officially a Chess Williams expert now. I know everything about him, and I can even prove it. Like, did you know that his favorite sandwich is chicken salad? Fascinating, right? And how about this little known fact—he actually loves basketball more than baseball! Which is so highly unusual, wouldn't you agree?" She shakes her head and rolls her eyes. "I'm sorry, I know I sound awful, but it's like, all she can talk about! Chess this, Chess that." She sighs. "Anyway, what's up with you and Teresa?" she asks, looking at me all sideways again. "You guys dating?"

"What do you mean?" I gaze at the busy street, noticing how almost all of the cars are driven by Bella Vista seniors, taking the long way home.

"Well, Jenay said you guys practically spent more time with each other than your dates. And then yesterday we tried to call you to ask you to come over, but your phone was off. I guess that's because you were helping her study. Or at least that's what I overheard you say at lunch. Are you guys like, good friends now?"

She's staring straight ahead, acting like it's perfectly okay with her that Jenay's ditched us for pep club and Chess, and that I'm supposedly best friends with Teresa. But I can tell it's really bothering her. And part of me wants to tell her about yesterday so she'll know there's nothing to worry about, that she and Jenay are still my best friends, and they won't be replaced. But the other part just wants to forget it ever happened. And in the end, that's the part that wins. "She sucks at math, so I helped her." I shrug.

"And Parker? Are you guys like, a couple now?" she asks, finally looking directly at me, her face a mix of worry and hope.

"I guess," I say, shrugging and smiling weakly.

"It's okay." She nods. "Really. I'm happy for you guys," she says, nodding again, this time more firmly.

I walk alongside her, running my index finger over the top of a neighbor's white picket fence. Thinking back to a time when things were so simple and easy.

"It's just . . . everything's changing," she says, staring far away.

"Tell me."

My mom left a note on the fridge, telling me how she and my dad are going to some faculty dinner party, but to go ahead and warm up the leftover lasagna and make myself a salad in case I get hungry.

I climb the stairs to my room, remove the jeans and sweater I wore to school, and replace them with my old, worn-out navy blue sweatpants, and my READING IS SEXY T-shirt that I ordered off the Internet mere seconds after seeing it on Rory Gilmore. Then I plop down on my bed and think about how I should probably be starting my homework even though I'd really rather not.

It's not often I get the whole house to myself, so I like to make the most of it when I do. Which usually translates to me just loafing around, wasting time, and not doing much of anything, since that seems to make the time last even longer.

It's weird how Jenay and Abby always get freaked out and scared when they're left home alone. Before their parents' car has even left the driveway, they're already on the phone, dialing everyone they know, trolling for company.

But not me. I totally love it. And I can't ever remember getting the slightest bit anxious or scared. Usually it's more the exact opposite. It makes me feel happy, expansive, and free. But that's probably because all last year my parents were like the gestapo, never allowing me more than a half hour's peace. And it's only in the last few months that they've finally begun to retreat.

I'm just about to turn on my iPod when my cell phone rings. And when I see that it's Parker my first instinct is to let it go straight into voice mail, even though I know that I shouldn't.

"Hey," I say, wedging it between my shoulder and cheek, trying to sound all upbeat and happy, like a good girlfriend would.

"What're you doing?" he asks.

"Um, nothing. Just lying here," I say, lifting my feet in the air, checking out my chipped-up pedicure, and thinking how I should probably cover it with some socks.

"Really?" he asks, sounding surprised.

"Yup, really," I tell him, adding no further comment.

"Who's all there?"

"Just me."

"You want company?" He laughs, but I can tell that he means it.

I roll over and gaze out the window. "You mean, now?" I ask, knowing he does, wishing he didn't.

"Yeah, I need a little help with my math homework and I hear you're the go-to math wiz."

"Oh really?" I say, laughing like I'm someone else, hoping I'll be mistaken for flirtatious.

"No, I just want to come over and hang. Is that cool?"

I stare at the oak tree, tall, dark, and barren. Then I roll back over and sigh. "Give me an hour," I tell him, closing the phone and reaching under the bed.

Fifteen

June 20

Last night my parents sat me down for a game of ulti-matum. Saying if I don't land a job by next Monday, then I'll find myself gainfully employed at the one they found for me. Some psych doc who needs a little help with filing and appt scheduling for all the sick heads that visit his office.

So of course I acted all offended, like it was way too beneath me to even consider. But the truth is, I'm thinking it could really work. Because, let's face it, making appoint-ments for the mildly insane definitely beats wearing a poly-ester uniform and hanging over a deep fryer, encouraging a nasty case of adolescent acne, or standing on my feet all day building bunions at some stupid, small-town boutique.

So now I can just screw around for the whole rest of the week, pretending I'm job hunting, and then Monday morning I'll show up fresh and eager and ready to report for duty at Dr. Freud's.

O yeah, Carly called last night, wanted to talk about what happened. I told her there's nothing to talk about, and wished her well. Then right before we hung up I just might have mentioned something about Stephen's annoying bicep-gazing-during-sex habit, and how she might want to look away when he eats since it's truly disgusting. And then I think she may have hung up on me. But, whatever.

Marc is as elusive and hard to reach as ever—which just makes me lust him even more! But I happen to know that he knows about Paula's party, so I'm wearing my cobalt blue halter top and white jeans in hopes that he shows.

June 23

Jeez—where to begin? Was it Lennon who said something about life being what happens when you're busy making other plans? Anyway, it's just so freaking true! I left the house around noon, dressed all conservative so everyone would think I was really going job hunting, when really I went straight to Paula's where I changed into my bikini and we spent all day reading magazines by the pool.

Then Kevin and Kristin stopped by (always together, together forever!), and by the time they finally split, Paula and I were so stoned we could barely move. Maybe that's the secret to their long-term romance, they're just way too messed up and unmotivated to go looking for someone else???

Anyway, before we even realized it, it was already getting dark, and all these people just started walking through the door, and we were still on our lounge chairs by the pool! And since it was Paula's party, and since she was all oiled up and still in her bikini, everyone just assumed it was supposed to be a moonlight pool party or something. So they just started stripping off their clothes and jumping in.

Including Paula who technically didn't have to get naked since she was already in a bikini, though I'm not really sure she realized that at the time. Anyway, I just lay there, making my way through a bag of chips, while my eyes searched for Marc, trying not to be too bummed out by the fact that I didn't see him anywhere, and trying not to care that everyone around me was all happy and hooked up, well, everyone but me.

So finally I decided to go into the house and look for something to change into, and I could not freaking believe it when I go past the den and see Marc sitting there, all alone, in front of the TV. Only the TV was off, and his eyes were closed. So I just assumed he was probably sleeping, stoned, or meditating or something. And I just stood there staring at him, thinking how peaceful and beautiful he looked being all still and mellow like that, but also wishing he'd open his eyes and see me.

But when he finally did, it was like nothing registered. He just sat there all silent, and then after awhile (which felt like forever) he finally patted the cushion beside him and passed me his iPod. And we sat there for like the longest time, just listening to music, and passing the earpiece back and forth.

And even though it was cool, and calm and really pretty nice, after awhile I started to get a little annoyed at how there I was, sitting right next to him, in my bikini, and all he wanted to do was listen to music by bands I've never even heard of! I mean, not to be stuck up or anything, but most guys are willing to drop way more than their iPods when I'm half naked and ready to go.

So finally, I just got up and left, thinking for sure he'd follow. Only he didn't. And when I finally got over myself and went back in the den, he was gone. And after searching the entire house, I realized he really was gone.

And I thought—screw him! But mostly I was feeling rejected. I mean, what's with this guy? What's with the whole mysterious Mr. Enigma act?

Anyway, I got changed, got myself together, and got myself home. And then later, just as I'm falling asleep, I see this flash in my window. Kind of like an SOS or something, even though I'm not really sure how that SOS flash signal really goes. But it seemed like a flashlight being turned off and on, slowly, with short spaces of darkness in between.

So, feeling kind of annoyed, and also kind of scared—I mean, was it aliens? Some psycho mass murderer? Because who does that? I got out of bed and headed for the window, moving the curtains just a tiny bit. And when I peeked through the narrow opening, I immediately grabbed my cell phone and started dialing 911. But then I looked again and I just couldn't freaking believe what I saw. It's like I seriously had to blink my eyes a whole bunch of times. I even rubbed them like you see in cartoons. But still, every time I opened them again, I saw the exact same thing.

So I creeped down the hall, and into Echo's room, being careful not to wake her. Then I went out to her balcony, and gestured in a what-the-hell-do-you-want kind of way. But he just stood there, motioning for me to come down.

And I thought—No effin way! This guy is totally whacked and he's probably planning to knock me out with his iPod Nano and drag me away, or something.

But then he kept waving, and then he smiled. So I grabbed hold of a branch, and made my way down the oak tree, just like I'd done a gazillion times before.

And when he met me at the bottom I asked, "What're you, crazy?" And I tried to look mad and not scared like I really felt. I mean, it just then occurred to me how the front door was locked and how I'd never be able to get back up the tree in time, you know, in case I was in danger or something.

But he just looked at me and goes, "I forgot to play you this one song."

And I just stood there, looking at him like he was completely looped. I mean, what the hell? It was like two o'clock in the morning. But still, I just stood there, listening to the song. It was jazz, and it was beautiful, though I'd definitely never heard it before. Then I gave him back his earpiece, praying to every god from every religion, begging to please just let me get back to my room safely and away from this music-loving head case who I mistakenly thought I liked.

And just as I started to climb back up the tree, he placed his hand on my shoulder, forcing me to face him. Well, my first instinct was to scream, but I didn't want to wake everyone and risk facing a world of hurt and a severely stunted summer, so I just turned around calmly, hoping I could talk him out of whatever sick act he was planning to perform.

And that's when he leaned in and kissed me!

It was only once. And it was really brief. But still, it was the most amazing thing that ever happened to me.

And then he smiled.

And then he left.

And I just stood there on the lawn, shivering in my bare feet, cotton cami, and boxers. Watching as he sprinted across the wet grass, leaving dark footprints in his wake, until I could no longer see him.

June 24

Today, when Echo walked in the door, holding the mail, she had the weirdest expression on her face.

"So bizarre," she said.

And I go, "What's bizarre?" And then I barely even looked up because I was busy eating strawberry yogurt while pretending to search through the want ads.

And she goes, "This. It was sitting in the mailbox."

And she tosses this packet on the table in front of me and it makes this kind of rattling sound as it lands and skids.

So I pick it up to see what the heck it is, and I go, "Huh, weird. It's some kind of seeds."

And she goes, "What kind of seeds?"

So I turn it over and see a picture of a tree on front. And it looks a lot like our oak tree does in the middle of spring, when its branches are all filled in with leaves. And then I see in the bottom of the left hand corner, in very small writing, the hand-scrawled words—Lush Life. And I remember the song from last night. The one Marc shared with me at two in the morning.

And Echo goes, "Who would put seeds in the mailbox?"

And I looked at her and smiled and said, "These are for me."

I close the diary and close my eyes, my mind drifting back to the day I found the packet of seeds in the mailbox, and how strange it all seemed at the time. And how Zoë's reaction made it seem even stranger, the way she smiled so secretly, like it actually meant something to her. Something she intended to keep from me.

I guess having been born just two years apart allowed me to take her for granted. Assuming she'd always be there, that nothing could take her away. I mean, right from the beginning she was always there to cheer me on and teach me everything she'd learned during her two-year head start.

It was Zoë who taught me how to keep my balance on my bike the day they took away my training wheels. And it was she who showed me how to build the perfect Barbie biodome subdivision using some old cardboard shoeboxes and a striped flannel sheet.

But now, thinking back on all that, I also remember how

when she moved away from all of those childhood things, she also moved away from me.

And it's weird how reading her diary is kind of like getting a second chance, like one last shot at knowing the sister who'd been so loving yet elusive, especially during those last few months.

I prop my pillows against my headboard, until it's comfortable enough to lean against. Then I reach for Zoë's diary and flip through the pages, picking up where I left off.

June 27

At first I thought I'd take those seeds and plant them right underneath my window. You know, as an act of charity for some future generation, some yet-to-be-born teenage girl who won't have to sneak down the hall, looking for escape, like me. But now that three days have passed and Marc hasn't even bothered to call, I think I'll probably just dump them in the trash, and try to forget the whole sick thing ever happened.

I mean, why hasn't he called??

Maybe he really is crazy.

Maybe I should just hang up on him when (if) he does.

June 28

Hung by the pool with Paula all day, just working on my tan. All she could talk about was her crush on Keith, determined to get to the bottom of who he looks like more—Russell Crowe or Ben McKenzie? Boring! I just pretended to be asleep.

I know I'm being a bad friend, but what can I say? Marc still hasn't called, and because of that I've decided to take a vow of mental celibacy. That's right. No more thinking about, dreaming about, or even talking about guys.

Any guys.

Because they're all the same.
They all suck.

June 30
Still celibate.
Still hate guys (with the exception of Dad—well, most of the time).
Extremely tan though.

July 2
Omigod. Where to begin? OK, started my job at the head shrinker today—way way better than I thought, though it's not like I'll be confessing that anytime soon. As far as my parents are concerned he's a fair yet firm employer, who has exceedingly high expectations that I will struggle to meet, and that's the story I'm sticking to.

When the truth is he spends most of the day behind a closed door, listening to all those messed-up whiners drone on and on about their lonely, miserable, fucked-up lives.

Which means my day is filled with long, leisurely fifty-minute breaks where I can nap, talk on my cell, surf the Net, whatever, just as long as the filing gets done and the phone answered within the first three rings. Not bad for a summer job.

But today I mostly napped. Because I was sooooo tired from last night. And here's why—

I was in my room, watching TV with the volume down low, when I heard someone calling my name. Not like yelling it out or anything, more like a loud—okay, really loud—whisper. So I immediately jumped up, ran to the mirror, combed my fingers through my hair, dabbed on some lip gloss, and sprayed some perfume, the whole time my heart beating so fast I thought it would break through my chest.

And then right as I started to run to my window, I stopped and thought—What the hell? He doesn't call for over a week, and now he shows up at one in the morning expecting me to do the whole Rapunzel thing again? Well, screw him.

So I plopped right back down on my bed and lifted the remote, ready to turn up the volume and tune him out. But then he called my name again and I started to worry that he was gonna wake the whole house, so I opened my window and faced him.

"Shhh!" I said, pressing my finger against my lips and shaking my head so he'd know that I meant it.

But he just raised his arm, the one holding the bouquet of flowers.

So I slipped down the stairs and out the front door, running all the way across the lawn to meet him.

"Here," he said, handing me the flowers he probably clipped from my next-door neighbor's yard. And when I brought them to my nose their smell was so sweet, it was hard to stay mad.

"What's going on?" he said, all casual, like everything was totally normal and not at all weird.

I just looked at him, as gorgeous and sexy as ever, but seemingly unaware of the fact that it was the middle of the night! "Um, what's going on?" I said. "Well let's see. It's after midnight, I haven't heard from you all week, and now you decide to just drop by and yell out my name 'til you wake the whole house." I shook my head and looked at him, trying my best to appear really mad.

But he just shrugged. "I don't have your number," he said.

So I go, "OK, well, you could've asked somebody for my number, you know, like Paula, or someone?"

But he just goes, "I don't have Paula's number either."

Then, "Listen, I was up at the lake, at my grandmother's house, and I didn't get back until late."

I just looked at him. He didn't seem like the kind of guy to hang with his grandma. So I go, "Please, your grandmother's house?" Then I shook my head, rolling my eyes for emphasis. And then I realized that I really didn't have a good reason not to believe that, other than the fact that it just seemed like a lie. "OK so why are you here now?" I asked, holding the flowers tightly to my chest, my heart pounding like crazy.

"Because I wanted to do this," he whispered.

Then he leaned in and kissed me.

And when he pulled away he reached into his pocket and grabbed a pen. Then he pushed up his sleeve and held out his arm. "Here," he said. "Write down your number so I can call you. And write big so I can see it in the dark."

And when I was done, he flipped open his phone and walked away. And by the time I made it back to my room, mine was ringing. And we talked for so long, I had to plug it into my charger. And he told me so many things, and answered so many questions, I don't think I've ever known anyone as well as this. Seriously, he even told me about how . . .

Crap. I drop the diary and listen to the doorbell ring. One time, quickly followed by two. Gotta be Parker. And I hate to admit this, but I wish he'd just go away so I can finish reading about Zoë and Marc and how it all began. It's like, in the beginning they were so much in love, but then later, they were a lot less so. And I need to know what happened in that space between, learn exactly what it was that made everything change.

But then the bell rings again, and I push the diary back under my mattress, gazing at the tree outside, and wondering if I should try to rappel my way down and run across the lawn just like Zoë would've done. I mean, it definitely seems a lot more romantic than making my way downstairs, opening the front door, and letting him in the usual way.

But then again, I'm not Zoë.

Which means I don't even stop by the mirror to check my reflection before I go downstairs to greet him.

Sixteen

I've never cooked dinner for anyone before, much less a guy. Though to be honest, I guess I still haven't. I mean, my mom's the one who actually *made* the lasagna. All I did was reheat it.

"This is excellent," Parker says, taking another bite.

"Glad you like it." I nod, hating the way I sound so stiff and formal, and how it's practically impossible for me to ever relax and be normal around him.

"I had no idea you were such a good cook." He smiles. "Which makes me wonder what other talents you're hiding."

I reach for my glass and sip my water, even though it's really more about nerves than thirst. "Well actually, I didn't really make it. You know, the lasagna," I say, mentally rolling my eyes at my lame-brain self, wondering what the heck he's even doing here. I mean, is he desperate? Is this some kind of bet?

"Well, you've got the whole reheating gig down, and that's gotta count for something, right?" He smiles.

We mostly talk about school, classes, teachers, people we know. And every time there's a break, every time it gets silent, the scraping of his fork sounds so incredibly loud that I say just about anything to fill up the gap.

He helps me clear the table, then I lead him to the den. But just as I make a beeline for the couch he touches my arm and goes, "Where's your room?"

And I go, "Oh, um, it's upstairs." Then I point in that direction, like he doesn't know where *up* is. *Oh God.*

"Can I see it?"

I glance at the clock, then back at him, knowing my parents won't return for at least another hour. Which technically should make me want to say *yes*, even though I'm a lot closer to *no*.

"Come on. I just wanna see what it's like," he says, smiling in a way that's trying a little too hard to seem friendly and harmless, and like he has no ulterior motives.

If I was Zoë, I would've served the entire meal on my bed, sitting Indian style on my duvet, with plates and dishes spread all around, just lighting candles, cranking a CD, and not giving a shit if anything spilled. But even though I'm nothing like her, that doesn't mean I have to act like me. So I grab his hand and take a deep breath, promising myself it will all be okay.

He stands in the doorway, scoping it out. "Yup," he says, making his way across the room until he's standing before my bookshelf.

"Yup, what?" I ask, leaning against the wall and trying to see my room for the very first time, to see it like he sees it.

His eyes scan the titles of all of my books, as his fingers brush lightly over my softball trophies, second and third place, from fourth and fifth grade. "Just like I thought," he says, turning to smile.

I just stand there, wondering if I should feel more disappointed that I'm apparently so predictable and easy to read.

"Lots of books, a few CDs, but thank God no puppy posters or pictures of Aaron Carter." He laughs.

"Well, I got rid of all that on my fifteenth birthday. Dumped it right in the trash. I'm into older men now. You know, octogenarians. Know where I can find a good Harrison Ford centerfold?" I ask, going over to lean on the edge of my desk and smiling nervously.

He checks out my TV, my iPod dock, and my bulletin board full of cards and letters and photos, including the one of me, Jenay, and Abby, making faces and hamming it up for the camera, and the one right next to it of Zoë and me sitting at the kitchen table, heads close together, crossing our eyes and sticking our tongues out at my dad, who was taking the picture. Then he wanders over to my bed, and sits on the edge. "When're your parents coming back?" he asks, trying to sound casual, like he's only mildly interested in the answer.

"An hour, two at the most," I say, gazing down at my feet and my messed-up pedicure, and then curling my toes under so he won't see.

"Would they freak if they found me here?"

I shrug. I mean, I really don't know the answer to that since it's not like I've ever had the opportunity to risk that kind of trouble before.

"No worries," Parker says. "If they come home, I'll just jump off your balcony." He nods toward my open french doors. "Or scale down that tree." He smiles.

Then he pats the mattress like a silent invitation, and I take a deep breath and move toward him.

We're kissing. We're lying on my bed and kissing. And I can taste the lasagna lingering on his tongue, and smell the garlic mixed in with his breath. And even though it's not near as bad as it sounds, it's not what you'd call "amazing" either.

Still, I'm going through the motions, moving my lips against his and running my hands through his hair, even though all the while I can't help wishing it was just a little bit better, just a smidge more romantic than it actually is.

But maybe it will never be like that for me. Maybe I'm not the kind of girl who inspires guys to spontaneous midnight visits and secret-message gift giving. Maybe I'm just like all the other girls who pretend they're content with *this,* when really they're longing for something more.

So far Parker hasn't tried to do anything more than just kiss, which mostly makes me glad. And the only reason I say *mostly* is because I'm hoping he's just trying to be cautious and respectful, and *not* because he's turned off by my dowdy sweatpants and tee.

I know I should've brushed my hair. Or at the very least, smeared on some lip gloss. I mean, we've been dating for less than a month, and I've already let myself go.

I move in closer, kissing him harder, and shifting my body so I'm lying on top of his. Then I squeeze my eyes shut and dream of another place, one where he's not really him, and I'm no longer me.

I run my fingertips down the side of his face, imagining his long dark lashes resting against his high, chiseled cheekbones. And when I reach up to brush my hair out of the way, I pretend that it's smooth, wavy, and rich, not limp, lank, and dull.

"Echo," he says, rolling me off 'til we're facing each other, lying again on our sides.

"Hmmm," I mumble, my eyes still closed, feeling happy and dreamy and free.

"Open your eyes," he whispers.

So I do. Slowly lifting my lids, until I'm startled by the sight of his golden blond hair and blue eyes, so different from the familiar, dark stranger I held in my mind.

"Should I go?" he asks, gazing at me, before leaning in to kiss the side of my cheek.

I squint at him, wondering why he's asking.

"Your parents. They'll be back soon, and I don't want you to get in trouble. I was just joking about scaling down your tree, you know that, right?"

But of course you were, I think, feeling disappointed that we're back to being us, so different from who I really want to be. And just as I roll over, and start to get up, Zoë's diary slips from its hiding space, and lands hard at my feet.

"What's that?" he says, reaching down to retrieve it.

But luckily I'm closer, which makes me quicker as well. So I swoop it up and hold it tight to my chest, then I look at him and say, "I think you should leave."

Seventeen

All day at school I went through the motions—nodding, smiling, taking notes, acing pop quizzes, waving to friends, eating lunch, acting cute with Parker by sharing my brownie and laughing at all of his jokes. Yet the whole entire time, my eyes were searching for Marc. And I found myself lingering in the hall where he smokes, leaning against the wall where he eats, and stopping to tie my shoe in the area just outside the girl's bathroom where I ran into him that very first day.

And it's not like I was planning to actually talk to him or anything. I mean, I didn't even know what to say. It's more like I just wanted to see him, be near him, and share the same space with this person who I know so much about, but in such a strange, remote way.

And all the while, for the whole entire day, I was just waiting for the bell to ring, knowing that's when I could finally go home, lie on my bed, pick up Zoë's diary, and take up from where I left off.

Even last night after walking Parker to the door, I had every intention of bolting back up to my room and reading the diary. But then my parents drove up, and my dad, his face all flushed and happy from an evening of intellectual conversation and one too many glasses of wine, insisted we hang out in the den, watch a little TV, and get reacquainted during the three-minute commercial breaks.

And by the time I finally snuck out of there, it was late, I was tired, so I decided to call it a night.

"Are you guys going?" Jenay asks, shifting her books and stopping, having just reached the corner where we say good-bye and head our separate ways. "You know, to Teresa's party?" she adds, removing a piece of windblown blond hair from her lip gloss and tucking it back behind her ear.

I just shrug and look at Abby. I mean, it's not like Teresa actually invited me or anything. But then I guess it's not really that kind of a party. It's more the haphazard, last-minute kind. The kind that gets planned the moment someone's parents unexpectedly head out of town.

"I heard it's going to be couples only. So count me out," Abby says, staring off toward our street.

"Are you serious? Just couples? That's so elitist," I say, shaking my head and laughing, trying hard to appear like my normal, slightly sarcastic self, so my friends won't see just how much I'm changing, and how I no longer care about any of this, especially now that I prefer Zoë's world to my own.

"I think that's only to keep the head count in check, so it doesn't get all crazy and out of control. So no excuses, Ab. I mean, it's not like there's gonna be a velvet rope and a bouncer, so it's not like you'll get turned away at the door. At least think about it before you say no," Jenay says, nodding encouragingly. "Please? Besides, if you want a date, I have the perfect guy all lined up and ready to go. All you have to do is say the word."

"Forget it," Abby says, blushing furiously but standing her ground. "I don't accept donations, hand-me-downs, charity dates, or mercy hookups."

"But you haven't even met him! At least think it over, before you go all negative on me," Jenay says, rolling her eyes but still laughing. "Listen, this guy is perfect for you, and this isn't some crazy, random pairing because I've actually been thinking a lot about this. He's super nice, really funny, and he's incredibly smart too. And I mean like, majorly smart. He's in my history class and he's never once stumbled when he gets called on. Seriously, even when he's messing around, he still knows *all* the answers."

Abby puts her hand on her hip and shakes her head. "Did you even listen to your list? Nice, funny, smart, super smart even! Oh lucky day for me! But did you say hot? No. Gorgeous? *Niente.* Cute? Not so much. That's a really bad sign, Jenay. A really bad sign." She narrows her eyes.

But no way is Jenay giving up. "But that's the thing, he *is* cute. Seriously, I swear. And the only reason I didn't mention it first is because I know you're not at all shallow or superficial. I know for a fact that you would never, ever base your opinion on looks alone." She looks at each of us, smiling triumphantly, knowing there's no way for Abby to argue with that.

Abby just stands there, squinting at Jenay as she mulls it over. "What's his name?" she asks, as though that will somehow reveal which way to go.

"Jax. Jax Brannigan."

"Jacks? Like plural? Like there's two of him?" Abby says, her eyes going wide, as her head moves back and forth, indicating an immediate, "no way in hell" decision. "Jacks the nice, funny, super incredibly smart, *two-headed history buff?*"

"Jax with an *x*. And you can't hold his name against him since it's not like he named himself," Jenay says, rolling her eyes, clearly frustrated with all of the obstacles Abby insists on throwing onto the otherwise well-marked path of love.

"What would you name yourself?" I ask, suddenly interested in this conversation, but probably only because as far as weird names go, I'm the undisputed queen. "I mean, if you could have any name, what would you pick?"

Abby laughs. "Well, when I was seven I wanted to be named Candy. So my dad started calling me Junior Mint, and my mom started calling me Abba Zabba and Aaron started calling me Twizzler, until I begged them all to please just stop and call me Abby again."

Jenay smiles. "I always wanted a cute name. You know, one that ended in an I or E sound." She shrugs. "But as it turns out, Jenay's a family name. So I'll probably be expected to pass it down someday too. You?"

Abby and Jenay both look at me, obviously curious how you could possibly ever top a name like Echo. And even though the years from kindergarten through fifth grade were the worst, with all the boys chasing me around, going, "Echooooo! Echoooo!" I guess I never really thought about changing it, never once thought about being anyone else—until now. I look at Abby and Jenay and just shrug.

"Well, I gotta get home and babysit. Call me if you guys get bored and want to come over. And Abby, think about it. Please, I'm begging you. I promise you will not be disappointed," Jenay says, turning down her street as Abby and I head for ours.

"Are you and Parker going?" she asks, gazing at me briefly, then down at the ground.

"Where? The party?" I look at her. "I don't know, I guess."

"Do you think I should go?" She gazes at me, her face set and serious, like she wants me to be serious too.

"Sure, if that's what you want." I shrug.

"I mean with Jax?"

"Again, up to you," I say, not feeling nearly as gung ho on the possibility of love like the ever optimistic and happy Jenay.

"Listen," Abby says, stopping in front of my driveway and gazing at me. "I don't mean to sound strange or anything, so I hope you don't take it that way, but . . . what's it like having a boyfriend? I mean, is it weird?" She scrunches up her nose and looks at me.

"What do you mean?" I ask, gazing down at the hole in the toe of my black Converse sneaker, thinking how I need to either get a new pair or find a new look.

"Well, Jenay acts like it's so great, I mean, she even wrote 'Ms. Jenay Williams' on her notebook the other day. Seriously. And when she saw that I saw she turned bright red and scribbled over it. But like, while she always acts so love happy, you . . . well you're like the exact opposite. You're like some big-time reluctant girlfriend, who can't quite figure out how you got there." She laughs at the end of that, but only to soften the blow.

I take a deep breath and stare at the crack in my driveway, surprised to learn I wasn't putting on near as good a show as I thought. Though I guess it's hard to fool Abby. I mean, she knows me too well. "Truth?" I finally say, looking right at her. "Just between us?"

She nods, waiting.

"It *is* weird. And to be honest, I really *don't* know how I got here. It just kind of happened, and before I knew it, I was in." I shrug.

"But weird how?" she asks, narrowing her eyes, obviously wanting to follow and understand. "I mean, what's it *like*? Do you talk on the phone all night? Are you going to have sex?"

I think about Parker, how cute he is, how nice he is, and I shrug. Honestly, I have no idea what he sees in me, no idea what he's even doing with me. But one thing's for sure, he's not the one who makes it so weird. That blame lies entirely with me.

I look back at Abby, then quickly glance away. Then I take a deep breath and say, "Honestly? Sometimes when he calls I purposely let it go into voice mail, because I feel so awkward, and nervous, and stupid, and guilty. And up until now we've only kissed or made out or whatever. But nothing more. I'm just not ready for more, and it's not like he pushes it, either. And it's like, even though I'm fully aware of how practically everything about him is really amazing and great, and even though I keep reminding myself of how lucky I am that he likes me, it's almost as though my heart refuses to cooperate with my head, like it's blocked out all of that chatter and refuses to listen. Does that make any sense?" I ask, wondering if she thinks I'm a total freak now that I've confided all that.

But she just looks at me and shakes her head. "You know what the sad thing is?" she says, still looking at me. "I think I can relate to your version a whole lot better than Jenay's." She laughs.

I laugh too. Then I head up the driveway, following along the thin, jagged crack 'til I reach the front porch.

"You wanna study later?" Abby calls out.

I reach for my keys and unlock the door. "Sounds good," I say, before closing it firmly behind me.

The moment I'm inside I bolt for my room, drop to my knees, and shove my hand under the mattress, wanting nothing more than to lie on my bed and get between the pages of Zoë's diary.

Only it's not there.

So I push my hand farther, delving deeper into the tight space where my mattress meets my box spring. And when it's still not there, I dive headfirst into full-blown panic attack.

Grabbing the pillows, sheets, blanket, and duvet, and throwing them all to the ground, I lift the mattress all the way up 'til the side is pointing at the ceiling, the top is resting haphazardly against my nightstand, and the entire left side wobbles like it's gonna crash through the french doors or something, as my eyes scan the space quickly, but not finding a thing. So then I drag it off completely, pulling it to the floor and flipping it over, thinking maybe the cobalt book got stuck to the stitching, but again, nothing.

I sink to the ground, a sweaty, panting, heart-racing mess. And as I unravel the sheet from my leg, my mind is in turmoil, wondering where the hell it could be, and even worse, who could've found it.

And when I finally gaze down, I notice how the sheet wrapped around my leg is *not* the same one I woke up with this morning. Since I know for a fact that when I left for school, I left behind an unmade bed with pink striped sheets. And these are cream with blue stars.

And then I remember Mariska. Our cleaning lady. The one who comes on the fifteenth of every the month. The fifteenth, just like today.

So I pick myself up and head for my dresser, Mariska's drop spot for orphaned items. And wouldn't you know, right there, smack dab in the middle, is Zoë's diary, cover shiny and blue, pages seemingly undisturbed.

Then I fix my bed, change my clothes, and begin where I left off.

   . . . *Seriously, he even told me about how he had to deal with his mom when his dad got shipped off to federal prison, how needy and weak she was, and how at just ten years old he was practically forced to grow up overnight.*

I'd always heard his family was mega, filthy rich, and supposedly had several more houses even bigger than the one he lives in now. And of course I'd heard all the crazy stories about his dad, but there were always so many rumors, so many insane legends—he killed a man, he robbed a bank, he embezzled a bunch of money, he was in the mob—that I just didn't know what to believe. So I didn't believe anything.

But I guess in the end, those stories were like a gazillion times more exciting than the true and boring fact of how his dad is just another greedy, rich bastard who wanted to be even richer.

Anyway, his mom ditched his dad, actually served him divorce papers during his first month in jail. Said there was no way she was living single for ten years minus time off for good behavior. So whenever Marc wanted to go see him, he had to get a ride with his uncle Mike (his dad's brother). And they'd both have to endure a full-body cavity search before they were allowed inside.

Only Marc didn't really say that part about the cavity search. He says that's how it is for hard-core criminals, not wealthy nonviolent types like his dad. Apparently all they had to do was sign in and go look for his dad—who, by the way, was allowed to wear clean pressed khakis instead of an orange jumpsuit. And then they all sat around at these plastic tables and chairs, eating vending-machine snacks and talking face to face (as opposed to being separated by a sheet of bulletproof glass and having to use a phone).

Whatever. My version's way better, way more dramatic. And I even told him he could show me a picture and I'd still choose to believe my story over his.

So he goes, "Oh yeah, and you're not allowed to take pictures either."

So I go, "See? In my version, they let you do that."

Anyway, I guess his mom became a major pill-popping heavy drinker, although she may have been one even before

*all that. I mean, it's kind of unclear but it really sounds like
it. And oh yeah, now she's apparently married to husband
number three, and each one has been even more rich (and
more messed up) than the one before.*

*So I went, "Is that why you drive that old Camaro,
cuz you hate money?"*

*But he just laughed and said, "I drive an old Camaro
cuz I like old cars. What, would you like me better if I
drove a Porsche?"*

*And then I—damn, I can't believe I said this (!) but
then I go, "I can't imagine liking you any more than I already do"!!!! Seriously! I could die! And I thought I
would! I mean it just slipped out before I could stop it.*

*But he just looked at me all serious and said, "I liked
you from the very first moment I saw you."*

*Which is kind of like "you had me at hello" but better,
because it's real, and spontaneous, and not from a movie.
So then I laughed, because, please, the first time he saw me
goes all the way back to fifth grade. Right before his mom
started sending him away to all of those private schools.*

*But when I reminded him of that, he just said, "I
know."*

Sometimes when I'm reading Zoë's diary I need to take little
breaks. I mean, part of me is anxious to move forward, and just
burn through the pages as fast as I can. But the other part feels
a little overwhelmed, like all of my senses are completely filled
up, and I just really need to set it down, close my eyes, and try
to regroup.

Though I guess I regrouped for too long, because the next
thing I know, the sun is set, my room is dark, and Zoë's diary
is gone.

"Who's there?" I sit up frantically, rubbing my eyes. "What

are you doing?" I ask, making an unsuccessful swipe for the book.

"What's this?" Abby asks, flipping through the pages, her eyes on the lookout for something good. "Are you holding out on me? Is this some kind of love journal, where you write down all of your heartfelt feelings for Parker?" She laughs, playing her version of keep-away.

I just look at her, forcing myself to take slow deep breaths, forcing myself to stay calm. "Abby, please. I'm serious. I really need that back," I say, struggling for patience as she scans the pages, though luckily without really reading. "Come on, Abby, please," I beg. "It used to be Zoë's."

I feel bad when it works. When I see her face go from gleeful to grave the second she hears my sister's name. But I had to get it back, and it's not like she left me with any other choice.

"I'm sorry," she says, shutting the book and handing it to me. "Honestly, I didn't know." She bites down on her bottom lip, her eyes wide and sad.

"It's okay," I say, sliding it back under my bed while giving her the "good sport" shrug. "Let's go study downstairs."

Eighteen

July 4
Fireworks! In the air, on the ground, vibrating all around
   Exploding in a profusion of color and sound
   We lay on the soft wet grass, staring up at a sky so lit
   A moment so perfect—I closed my eyes to save it—
   Then later, quiet, peaceful, just him and me
          Two hearts reaching for infinity.

Carly was pissed I didn't go to her party—assumed it was because of her being all happy and hooked up with Stephen. Please, I could give a shit about all that. I mean, seriously. Whatever. I tried to tell her I'd already made plans, but it just made it worse. She got all hostile and hurt and accused me of ditching her for Marc!

"You've totally changed since you hooked up with him!

You've ditched everyone else just so you can be with him," she yelled.

I just held the phone and rolled my eyes, because no way was I getting sucked into her self-righteous not-so-mellow-drama.

So then she goes, "Everyone's talking about it, and I'm only telling you this because you're my best friend and I love you like a sister."

"Oh, is that why you stole my boyfriend?" I asked, which I know was stupid since it's not like I care. I guess I just couldn't stand to listen to her stupid, fake, best-friends-forever-and-ever-and-ever bullshit speech, especially since it's no longer true.

So she goes, "You were over Stephen and you know it. I can't believe you're acting like such a bitch, over a guy!"

But I didn't say anything. Seriously, I refused to get sucked in any further.

So then she goes, "Seriously, Zoë, I'm worried about you. Everyone's worried about you. I mean, how well do you even know him? 'Cause I've heard some pretty scary stories about his private school years. Why do you think he had to enroll in public again? It's because he had no choice, nobody else would take him. Honestly, I think that whole quiet and mysterious act is totally played. Because the truth is, he's just weird. And I know you know what everyone says about his family, right? I mean, they're bad news. It's like, he shows up at parties, but then barely even talks to anyone. He's got all that money but he drives that old, beater car. He's like some rich-ass grease monkey, and his mom is like a total pharm-hound boozaholic, not to mention she's been married like a zillion times, not to mention how his dad's supposed to get out of jail anytime now and Marc will probably go live with him—a convicted felon! A former prisoner! I mean, have you even thought about any of this?"

I know I shouldn't have let her get to me, I know I should've just ignored it, but I couldn't just let all that go. So I said, "You don't know what you're talking about. Everything you just said is all rumors and bullshit! None of it's true! And if you were my friend then you would believe me, not judge me, and stand by me no matter what!"

But she just goes, "Sorry Zoë, but I just can't do that."

So I go, "Then you know what, Carly? I guess you're not really my friend."

When I hung up I felt pretty bad, I mean, we really did used to be best friends. But then I used to think I had a lot of friends. I used to think everyone loved me and cared about me, and only wanted the best for me. So it feels pretty bad to know they're all talking shit about me instead.

But still, if I'm forced to choose, and apparently I am, then I choose Marc. And it's not like I owe Carly or anyone else an explanation for that.

Because if you're gonna make someone choose, then you shouldn't be surprised when they don't choose you.

July 7
Almost got caught taking a catnap at work today. Big time, serious close call. Normally I'm way more careful about stuff like that—I even set the alarm on the computer for ten minutes before the appt ends. But I guess I just didn't hear it go off, cuz the next thing I knew Doctor Freud was standing over me, fingers scraping against his graying old scraggle chin, going, "Zoë? Are you okay?"

Luckily, I was slumped so far down my face was practically in my lap, so without even flinching I just opened my eyes, reached down, and grabbed the pen that had fallen on the ground. Then I looked up at him and smiled and said, "Yeah, I was just looking for this." Then I held up that blue ballpoint, like it was solid evidence of a hard day's work. And even though I don't really think he bought it, he still just nodded, and then headed for the can. And by the time he got back his next appt was already there.

But the truth is, I was exhausted from Marc. And the fact that he spent the night last night! Seriously—the whole, entire, wonderful, glorious, outrageous, world-changing, life-altering night!

Since Echo left for her annual "Cerebral Campers" week or whatever they call that Camp Brainiac thing she goes to every year, Marc scaled the tree, came in through her room, crept down the hall, and spent the whole night with me until I heard both my parents making their way down the stairs in the morning.

It was the first time we'd actually slept together, first time we had sex together! And even though we've been dating for only two weeks—well two weeks ago since the first time he kissed me, then he left me hanging for a while but still, he's pretty much the one that made us both wait. He said he didn't want to rush it, that we should give it time to build.

I gotta admit, that worried me at first. I guess because I always figured he'd slept with a lot of girls. I mean he's so hot, and so cool, and so sexy, and so mega rich, and definitely has that mysterious bad-boy vibe going. So I figured there were tons of ritzy, ditzy, country-club sluts just lining up to be with him. But he said he was done with all that, after his last girlfriend a little over a year and a half ago, and now, I swear this is what he actually said—Now all he wants is ME!

I wanted to believe that, but I kind of had my doubts. Also, I felt like I had to test him, so I could see if he really

wanted me for me, or for the me that he wanted me to be.
So I told him about all the guys I'd done it with, starting
with the blow job I gave Bryan Boxer back when I was
thirteen. And even though there really aren't all that many
guys (I mean thirteen was just three years ago), and I was
with Stephen for a full year and a half (minus the two times
I cheated) but still, most guys freak out at that kind of in-
formation, which is why most girls lie. Isn't it funny how
guys and girls always lie in opposite directions? Guys add,
girls subtract.

Anyway, Marc just lay there beside me, listening pa-
tiently, and when I was done, he just shrugged and said he
didn't care. "Each step brings you closer to the next," he
said. "And that's where we are now, the next step."

So then I asked him about the next step after me.

But he just kissed me on the forehead and said, "Shh.
All we ever have is now."

How could I feel good about my life after reading that? Seriously. How could I possibly settle for my super nice, but ultimately boring (fine, there, I finally said it, okay?) boyfriend,
and our low-to-no-passion makeout sessions, when I now
know (albeit secondhand) just what it's like to have the real
thing?

I mean, I know I should probably just set the diary down
and back away slowly, go cold turkey and never peek at it
again, since all it seems to do is feed my disappointment and
make me yearn to be someone and to have something that was
never meant to be mine.

But now that I'm so far in, I can't find my way out. And
the truth is, with what I now know, I don't ever want to go
back.

I have to break up with Parker. I mean, it's the right thing to do. Because staying with him, going through the motions, and pretending to be happy isn't fair to anyone, especially him. But I feel so inept, and inadequate, and meek, and stupid, that I'm just not sure how to do it.

Not to mention that I'm just not sure if I'm up for all the fallout. You know, all the wheres, whats, whys, and hows that'll ultimately follow. And what am I supposed to do at lunch? Do we still sit together, acting all amicable, while pretending it never happened? Or does one of us have to move? And if so, will it be me?

Nineteen

On the night of Teresa's party, Abby was no longer trying to play it cool. And after calling me like a ton of times trying to decide what to wear, she moved on to e-mailing me photos of her top three choices, all laid out and spread across her bed, with empty sweater arms waving hello, unfilled pant legs river dancing, vacant shoes pointing in every direction, while her most beloved childhood dolls and stuffed animals stood in for her head.

She'd decided to go with Jax. Ever since the day Jenay invited him to sit with us at lunch and he turned out to be not only nice, smart, and funny, but also pretty cute. And since technically this is Abby's first date, there's no way she's leaving anything to chance. Seriously, she has it all planned out. Even down to the conversations she expects to have.

I want to help her, really, I do. But my mind is totally stuck on Zoë's diary, as I skim through the pages and reread certain parts, reluctant to move ahead, not wanting it to end.

"Okay, so which is better?" Abby asks. "Winnie the Pooh wearing the white blouse, blue corduroy vest, and jeans? Or Lisa Simpson in the flowy blue skirt and sweater?"

"Neither. I'm liking the Bratz doll in the black sweater, black boots, and jeans," I say. "Although her head looks disproportionately small, and a bit lost inside that turtleneck. And that could make some of those well-scripted conversations more than a little bit awkward. Not to mention the kiss good night. So maybe you should switch to a V-necked sweater instead, you know, to even it out." I laugh.

But Abby's way too freaked to have a sense of humor. "Okay, that's it. I'm calling Jenay," she says, hanging up before I can even apologize.

I stare at the phone and think about Marc. Remembering how his number's still probably stored from that one time he called. And hating how I've been acting like such a wimp and determined to do something bold, I scroll down to his name and push *talk*. And before I can chicken out and hang up, he answers.

I sit on my bed, frozen, unable to speak. "Echo?" he says. "You okay?"

And I remember how the display works both ways.

"Um, yeah." I clear my throat while my fingers pick at a loose thread on my blanket.

"Where are you?" he asks, sounding calm, if not interested.

"Home," I mumble, wondering what to say next.

"So, how are you?" he asks, the background music growing softer as he turns it down.

"I miss her," I say, before I can stop.

He sighs. Then he says, "Wanna go for a ride?"

I would answer, but there's a speed bump in my throat, and it's stopping all my words.

But he doesn't need an answer. "I'll be right over," he says, before closing the phone.

I grab my purse and run downstairs, stopping by the kitchen just long enough to tell my mom that I'll be right back.

"Where are you going?" she asks, turning away from the sink just long enough to see what I'm wearing. For someone who was never much interested in fashion, she sure makes it a point to always take the time to check out my clothes now. But I guess that's just another lesson learned during the whole Zoë thing, and how the cops need that kind of information so they can fill in the "last seen wearing" box on the police report.

I pause long enough for her to get a good look, then I head for the door, yelling, "I have to run an errand, so I'll see you in a few." And before she can even respond, I'm out the door and sprinting toward the corner, hoping to meet up with Marc without anyone seeing.

And when he turns onto my street, and I see the shiny midnight blue of his restored Camaro glinting in the hard winter sun, I feel happier than I can ever possibly explain.

"Hey," he says, as he leans across the seat and props open the door.

I settle onto the black leather, noticing how the interior feels deeper and darker than my parents' cars, almost like a cave. And I remember how Zoë used to call it The Coffin, and how that used to be funny, but not anymore.

"Park okay?" he says, glancing at me before pulling away from the curb.

I just nod and gaze out the window, feeling excited for the first time in days.

We don't really talk along the way, we just listen to music by some band I've never heard. And when we get there, he parks the car and reaches behind my seat, the sleeve of his brown leather jacket brushing against mine. Then he tosses me a bag of breadcrumbs and we head for the lake, where the ducks are already gathering, waiting to be fed.

I settle onto the grass beside him and start tossing crumbs, wondering if the view looked better to Zoë, less polluted, more serene, like maybe being in love somehow improved it.

"I'm reading it," I finally say, knowing I owe him an explanation for pulling him away from his day. But my throat feels tight, and my eyes start to sting, and it's hard to say more, so I don't.

But he just looks at me. "I know."

I glance at him, wondering how.

"You called. And you're no longer angry." He shrugs.

"I was never angry," I say, pulling my hand away from an overly aggressive beak.

"Just give him the rest, so they'll all go away." He laughs.

I empty the bag and bite down on my lip, feeling this weird sense of comfort sitting so close to him, someone who I know so much about, and who knows that I know.

"How're your parents?" he asks.

I just shake my head and shrug.

"They still hate me?" He looks at me, eyes neither worried nor hopeful, just curious.

"Probably." I shrug. "You going to the trial?"

"Wouldn't miss it. I need to see that freak, I need to watch him pay. Couple more months though, right?"

"That's what they say." I watch the last duck, still pecking around near my feet, and I pull them in too so I won't lose a toe. "Thanks for bringing me here," I say, gazing up at him shyly. "I mean, I know this may sound weird and all, but being around you makes me feel close to her." I bite down on my lip, wondering how he'll take that.

But he just closes his eyes and lifts his face toward the fading sun. "Being here makes me feel close to her. That's why I come every day."

"Even when it rains?" I ask, trying to sound light and teasing, even though the moment is so clearly wrong for a joke. But that's what I do when I'm nervous, I make inappropriate, stupid jokes.

But he just sighs. "Every day feels like rain," he says, his eyes still closed, his long, thick lashes seeming almost fake the way they rest against his skin.

"Is your dad out?" I ask, wanting to change the subject, but suspecting this might not be the right way.

"Not yet." He shrugs.

"Will you live with him when he does get out?"

He shakes his head and looks at me. "I'm in the guest house now, it's like having my own place. So I plan to stay put until college."

"Where you going?" I ask, suddenly panicked at the thought of him leaving, especially now that I'm just getting to know him.

"Berkeley's my dream, Columbia would be cool, but my grades kind of suck, so probably right here."

"Don't say that," I tell him, even though part of me wants it to be true.

But he just shrugs. "Wanna grab a bite?" He looks at me.

I do. I really, really, really do. I want to go anywhere he wants to go. I'd follow him wherever, just to be with him. Only I can't. "I'm supposed to go to this party," I say, lifting my shoulders and rolling my eyes, trying to come off as grown up, world-weary, and jaded. But when he raises his eyebrows, I look away. Since it's obvious he still sees me as Zoë's little sister.

I wish he would notice how much I've changed, how the last year has shaped me, transformed me. But he doesn't. So I grab my purse and stand. "Can you drop me off? I need to go get ready," I say, my voice carrying an edge that's hard to miss.

He holds up his keys and they jangle together, then he stands and heads for the car.

And I walk alongside him, feeling small, silent, and frustrated. Wondering just what it will take to get his attention.

He comes around to my side, unlocking the door, and letting me in. And just as I start to move past him, my hip accidentally rubs against his, and his face is so close, and his eyes so deep, that I can't help but lift my fingers to his smooth, sculpted cheek. Then without even thinking, I close my eyes, lean in, and kiss him.

He hesitates at first, but only for a moment. Then he wraps his arms around me, pulling me tight against his chest, kissing me hard on the mouth, until he finally pulls away and whispers, "Echo, trust me, you don't want—"

But I do want. So I pull him back to me, leaving no room for questions, no room for doubt. Thinking this is exactly how a kiss should feel—glorious, heady, and intoxicating. Like those first three sips of vodka the night of the homecoming dance, only a gazillion trillion bazillion times better.

And even though I'm borrowing a moment from Zoë's life, one that will never truly be mine, at this moment I just don't care. I'm living for now.

"Echo," he whispers, pulling away, calling my name even though I'd rather be Zoë. "Echo, stop."

I open my eyes and smile, at first not noticing the dark cloudy look in his. But the moment I see it, I follow their trail.

And at the end stands Teresa.

Twenty

"Are you sure this is okay?" Abby whispers, for like the hundredth time since she and Jax arrived.

"Omigod, it's fine," Jenay says, rolling her eyes and laughing. "Seriously, you look amazing."

"Echo?" Abby looks at me. "Hello! Earth to Echo? Any comments on my outfit? Do these jeans make me look fat? C'mon, you can tell me, I can take it."

I look at her and force myself to smile. "Please, you couldn't look fat if you tried. Really. Now the Bratz doll? *She* looked fat. She just couldn't pull it off like you can."

Luckily Abby and Jenay both laugh, which means I'm pulling it off better than I thought. They have no idea how I'm not really here, that in my head, I'm back in the parking lot with Marc, just seconds after we both saw Teresa.

We didn't speak the whole way home, but when he stopped on my corner he turned to me and said, "Echo, I'm so sorry. I—"

"Don't." I stared straight ahead, listening to the steady hum of the engine, determined to be brave and say what I felt for a change, rather than chickening out and running away like usual. "Don't apologize," I said, turning toward him. "I wanted to see you. And I'm not at all sorry for what happened." I felt stronger after saying that, strong enough to actually look him in the eye.

"And Teresa?" He looked at me, his eyes filled with worry.

I took a deep breath, remembering the expression on her face, the wide eyes and gaping mouth so easy to translate, even from all the way across the parking lot. And how it turned into a slow curving smile as she watched us climb into the car and drive away. "I'll deal with Teresa," I said, having not the slightest idea how I'd actually do that. But it sounded convincing.

Then I grabbed my purse and crawled out of the car, shutting the door firmly between us. And just as I started to move toward my house, I turned back, leaned through the open window, and said, "Hey Marc, thanks. Thanks for today."

He smiled at me, holding my gaze for a moment. Then he turned up his stereo, shifted into gear, and drove away.

But now, with the three of us crowded into Teresa's guest bathroom for the sole purpose of talking Abby down from her self-induced, body-dysmorphic panic attack, I realize I still have no plan for how to handle Teresa.

But then again it's not like she doesn't have her own secrets to hide. And it's not like she was alone either.

"Listen, this is crazy. We've got to get out of here," Jenay says, having reached her limit as she reaches for the door handle.

"We're in here, the guys are out there, and there's something very wrong with this picture. Abby, you look great, you *are* great, and I can tell Jax is totally into you. But if you don't get out of this bathroom right this second and back to your date I'm going to scream."

Abby takes a deep breath and follows Jenay, while I linger behind the two of them, peering into the mirror as they head out the door, wondering how it's possible to still look like me, when I feel so different inside.

Okay, so normally on a Saturday night, when someone's parents are out of town and they decide to throw a party, you can pretty much expect to see the usual things—music blaring from somebody's docked iPod, a lamp and/or vase breaking into a million little pieces, a half-hearted fistfight that breaks up well before they can take it outside, sporadic alcohol-induced vomiting in the bushes, people sneaking upstairs to hook up—I mean, those are just some of your basic, all-purpose party ingredients, right? Not that I've been to that many parties, but still, I've watched a lot of TV and movies and read a lot of books, so I think I know what to expect.

But Teresa's party is nothing like that. Probably because she only invited her friends from school, which means she's acting more like her *lunch table* self—you know, cute, flirty, preppy, and fun, as opposed to her *off-campus* self—the slutty girl who smokes and drinks, wears low-cut sweaters, and has really bad taste in men. I mean, if "Hot Jason" and "Asshole Tom" were here, I doubt she'd be blasting the indie girl CD, serving snacks and appetizers from a carved, bamboo tray, and dispensing cocktails from her parents' sleek, well-stocked, mahogany bar.

It's like everything is so carefully coordinated—the plates match the cups match the napkins match the flowers—heck, even her outfit is in cahoots, with the belt, shoes, and earrings all coordinating with tonight's color scheme. And it's kind of bizarre to be hanging with a bunch of kids from school on a Saturday night, at a party that seems way more like a baby shower.

"I saw this same exact spread in *InStyle* magazine," Teresa says after Jenay compliments her on the tiny, matching, sky-blue bud vases she placed in an undulating pattern across the glass-topped coffee table. "It was for someone's baby shower, I can't remember who. Jennie Garth? Jennifer Garner?" She scrunches up her face. "No, someone else. Anyway, I clipped it because the second I saw it I knew I wanted my baby shower to be just like that, but then I thought, omigod, what am I waiting for? I mean, getting knocked up is like, at least a decade away. So I just made a few tweaks, and *voilà*!"

She says *"voilà!"* like "voy-la!" But I don't have the heart to correct her. I just stand there, sipping my drink and smiling, wondering if she has any immediate plans to out me.

I gaze over at Abby who's perched on the edge of the sofa, nodding at Jax's every word, and trying hard to look interested in whatever it is that he's saying. And then Parker walks up, slips his arm around my waist, and kisses me on the cheek.

And my eyes dart straight for Teresa, like the second he does that, wondering what she'll do. But she just smiles even wider and goes, "You guys are way too cute together." Then she winks at me and walks away.

"Come on, I wanna show you something," Parker says, tugging on my arm as he leads me upstairs. And when we end up in the guest room, well let's just say I'm not exactly surprised.

"Parker, I don't think—" I start, but then he puts his finger over my lips before quickly replacing it with his mouth.

So I let him kiss me. At least while we're still just standing by the door. But when he tries to pull me toward the bed, I shake my head and go, "No." Pulling away, attempting to free myself from his grip.

"Come on." He smiles. "No one's gonna walk in. It's just us."

But it's not about somebody walking in. It's about the fact that I just can't do this anymore. Not after having kissed Marc. Not after having tasted the real thing.

"I just want to go back downstairs and hang out with my friends," I say. "Come on, let's go. We can do this later."

"*I'm* your friend," he says in this syrupy voice that totally gets on my nerves. "And I'm right here."

"I mean my *other* friends. You know, like Jenay and Abby and everyone else." I shake my head and roll my eyes, making no attempt to hide it.

"What's your problem?" He squints at me, his face looking more hurt than angry. "You hardly answer your phone, you're always running off. It's like, if you don't want to be with me, Echo, then just say it."

I gaze down at the ground, then back at him, wishing I could be the right kind of girl. The kind who wouldn't just *know* that she's lucky to be with him, but actually *feel* it too. The kind of girl he deserves. But I've strayed so far from normal now, I'll never find my way back. And the truth is, I no longer want to.

"I don't think we should do this anymore," I finally whisper, still staring at the ground, yet feeling the weight of his stare upon me.

He stands there for a moment, not saying a word. Then he shakes his head and brushes right past me. "Whatever," he says, as he heads down the stairs.

By the time I make it back down, it's pretty clear that everyone knows. I can tell by the way they all look at me, eyes wide, lips parted, voices gone suddenly silent. Believe me, if anyone knows the signs of being the headline, the star of the big juicy story, it's me.

So I head straight for the door, knowing better than to stay. And just as I grab the handle, Jenay and Abby appear. "Where you going?" they ask, their voices careful, their faces concerned.

"It's a couples party," I remind them. "And since I'm no longer a couple . . ." I shrug, wanting to leave it at that, but knowing I can't. They're my best friends, which means they've earned the right to hear more. "Listen, don't worry. I'm fine. Just have fun and call me tomorrow. I'll explain it all then, okay?"

And before they can even respond, I'm already halfway down the drive. And just as I reach the end I hear Teresa call out, "Hey Echo, be careful out there, okay?"

And I don't know if she's referring to the walk home, or what she saw at the park. But either way, I just keep going.

Twenty-one

July 10

I've never felt like this before. It's like, I thought I knew what it was like to be in love—the first time with Bryan Boxer, back in seventh grade, for one crazy, completely awkward week, and then again freshman year, when I first hooked up with Stephen (when I was young and impressionable and didn't know any better). But now I know I was wrong.

Dead Smacking Wrong.

THIS is love.

Marc is Love.

Me + Marc = love.

I know it sounds crazy since I'm only sixteen, but I just can't help but believe that we were made to be together. I mean it. I love everything about him. There's nothing that annoys me or gets on my nerves (a total miracle, I know). And whenever we're apart for more than a few hours, I feel this major aching loss, like I'm weak and incomplete, until we're finally back together again.

Okay, I just reread that last part and totally cringed. And to be honest, I'm thinking I should probably just scribble it out and pretend I never wrote it. I mean, WEAK and INCOMPLETE? Get a freaking life already! I know. But still, I'm just gonna leave it there, cuz the truth is, it's how I really feel. And even though I can't imagine ever not feeling this way, I still want to write it all down—the good, the bad, and the completely embarrassing—so that I can read it again someday, when we're both old and gray, swinging in a hammock and listening to our iPods—or whatever old people will do in the future.

Anyway, Marc's been sneaking into my room practically every night for the last week, but now with Echo coming back soon, we're gonna have to find another way. I mean, she probably wouldn't care if he tiptoed past her bed, since she's a pretty deep sleeper and it's not like she's ever busted me before, but I'm still not one hundred percent positive I even want her to know. I just don't think it's such a good idea to involve her in this. So I guess I'll just have to think a little harder, and find another way.

Yesterday I snuck him into work, and stashed him under my desk. It's a HUGE wood desk, so trust me, he fit. And we totally made out during one of the fifty-minute sessions. And then right before our time was up he kissed me good-bye and said, "I better get out of here before the goateed wonder catches us."

And as I sat back in my chair, I readjusted my skirt and said, "You gonna go look at that Camaro? The one you told me about?"

And he just nodded and went for the door.

Then right before he walked out I went, "Hey, how'd

you know he has a goatee?" And when I looked at him, I noticed he had the weirdest expression on his face, but then just like that it was gone.

And he goes, "You told me."

And then he left.

But the thing is, I don't remember telling him that, since I never really talk about my job to anyone other than my parents who insist on a weekly report so they can make sure I'm working hard as opposed to humiliating them in front of a colleague.

But I guess I must've told him, because how else would he know?

July 11

Marc picked me up from work today in his same old Camaro, saying that in person, the one he was gonna buy was just not up to his standards. Whatever. I mean, to me it's just some old beater car that takes up most of his free time, and I just don't get the attraction. But as long as he's willing to drive me to work and back, I guess I can't really complain. Not to mention how it spares me from having to beg for my own car, since my parents are pretty much not cooperating and refusing to hear my pleas.

Speaking of parents, I have to say that it's kind of weird how I've never met his mom. Not to mention how I've never even been to his house! I mean he's here all the time, and even though my parents definitely don't know about him spending the night and stuff, at least I've introduced them! Though I did try to keep it all casual and act like he was just a friend.

I'm still not sure why I did that, and I could tell Marc was kind of hurt. Even though he didn't really say anything other than, "Why'd you call me your friend?"

But I just said, "Cuz you are my friend. And believe me, it's not like they need to know all the details."

So we just left it at that, but still, I could tell he was bothered.

I guess there's just so many crazy, mean rumors about his family that I didn't want my parents to get all freaked or anything. I mean, I LOVE HIM, I really, really do. But that doesn't mean they'll understand.

July 20

Echo's back. Which means I've barely had time to see Marc since I've been working all day, and I've yet to figure a way to get him into my room without getting caught. And because of that, we had our first fight.

And I know how most people keep journals specifically for moments like this, but it drags me down so bad, I don't feel like writing about it, much less thinking about it. I guess that's why I didn't write for a few days, but we're better now, so I'm back.

But if I'm gonna be honest (and if I can't be honest here, then where?) then I have to say that it's just not the same as it was before. Now it's different, altered. Like when you scrape your knee and you get a scar, but then the scar fades so much that no one can see it but you. But you know where it is. Cuz you remember what caused it. And no matter how hard you try, you can never forget how bad it hurt when it first happened.

Well, that's how it is with us. From the outside, everything looks the same, but on the inside, it's all different. And what makes it even worse is that it was all my fault to begin with.

It's just, sometimes Marc gets so detached and quiet that it makes me all needy. And then needy turns to whiny. And then, well, I started nagging him about not having *enough time together (which is totally crazy, I know) but I was just hoping that would make him invite me over, even if his mom is half out of the bag all the time. I mean, he lives in a mansion, so it's not like she'll even notice.*

But he didn't invite me. He didn't say anything. So then, of course, I started accusing him of not wanting to be with me (I know, pathetic, insecure, lame, etc). Until he goes, "Zoë, I'm 16. What do you want from me?"

And I went, "NOTHING!" Which obviously was a lie. So then I said, "Do you realize that not once have you invited me to your house?"

And he closed his eyes and shook his head, which only egged me on more.

So I go, "I'm serious. You've met my parents so why can't I meet yours?" Which I know is not exactly fair since that time when I first introduced them I didn't really cop to our relationship, instead I pretended we were study buddies.

But then he looked right at me and said, "Trust me, you so don't want to come to my house."

And I said, "You don't know what I want."

So then he shook his head and said, "Fine. But don't say I didn't warn you."

I lay in bed, with Zoë's journal facedown on my chest, watching the red message light on my cell phone flash on and off in my now darkened room. I know it's either Abby, Jenay, Parker, or Teresa. But it doesn't matter. My phone's been ringing off and on practically since I got home, but not once did I consider answering it.

I know my friends are probably just worried, and I know the least I can do is let them know I'm okay so I close the diary and pick up the phone, wondering just exactly where to start making amends.

But there's only one message, and when I hear it, I realize it's not really a message, just a bunch of music. And just as I'm about to delete it, thinking for sure it's a mistake, I remember the song from Marc's car, the one that was playing as he drove away.

And I lay there with the phone pressed tight to my ear, playing it over and over again, until I finally fall asleep.

Twenty-two

The next morning I'm listening to Abby's version of everything that happened, in sequential order, from the moment I left Teresa's party to the moment she left Teresa's party.

"So wait, Parker was flirting with who? I thought it was couples only," I said, phone clenched between my shoulder and ear as I paint my toenails a nice deep red. "Was he hitting on someone else's date?"

"Trust me, after you left, it all went to hell. And by ten o'clock word was out, and practically all of Bella Vista showed up."

"Seriously? What'd Teresa do? Whip out more cheese logs and little blue drink umbrellas?"

Abby laughs. "No. Always the perfect hostess, she just raided the liquor cabinet and the wine cellar. It got pretty crazy. I bet she's really gonna pay when her parents get home."

"I'm not so sure about that," I say, replacing the polish top and leaning down to blow on my toes. "I hear she's pretty spoiled, you know, only child, daddy's little princess, mommy's little protégée."

"Must be nice," Abby says. And then, "I mean, well, you know."

"Relax." I gaze out the window. "I may be the only child left, but I'm no princess. Anyway, back to you. You know you still haven't told me what I really want to hear. What happened with you and Jax? Disaster? Or love at second sight?"

Abby sighs loud and heavy, and for a moment she sounds much older than her years. "I don't know. He's cute, and nice, and all that, but when he walked me to the door and kissed me good night, well, there weren't really any sparks, you know? I mean, I know you can't always expect bottle rockets, but can't I at least get a sparkler?"

I think about the difference between Parker and Marc, and realize how funny it is that I, of all people, can now be considered some kind of expert. Well, at least where Abby's concerned. But then I remember how she doesn't actually know about Marc, at least not that I know of. "Did it seem kind of clinical?" I ask. "Or more like a relative? Like a frisky, drunken uncle?"

"That's disgusting, but no. It was more like two actors rehearsing a role, hoping they were getting it right. Like, the whole time my lips were moving my head was thinking, *That's it? You waited fifteen years for this?*"

"Yikes."

"Tell me," she says. "But here's the thing, do you think maybe it was just nerves? I mean, do you think I should try it again?"

And just as I'm about to answer, I get a new call. So I put Abby on hold, only to find Teresa on the other line.

"Hey," she says. "What're you doing?"

"Talking to Abby," I tell her, hoping that will speed it along.

"Dump her, I need to talk to you."

I roll my eyes. Apparently, now that she's got some dirt on me, she figures the usual pleasantries no longer apply. I guess she forgot how I saw her too. "She called first," I finally say.

"Fine. Listen, I was wondering if you wanted to come by and hang out. You know, so we can study." She laughs. "I hear you're really good at math."

I close my eyes and sigh. Teresa can really be a bitch, but apparently I'm the only one who knows it. "I'm busy," I say, anxious to get back to Abby.

"Yeah? Well, I think you might want to clear your calendar and try to stop by because Marc's coming over."

I just sit there, silent and still.

"In fact, he should be here within the hour."

Why is Marc going to Teresa's? I mean, they're not friends. At least not that I know of. And even though I could probably just ask and get it over with, I'm more than a little reluctant to give her the satisfaction. "We'll see," I finally say, trying to sound distracted and uninterested. "I've got a lot going on today."

"Door's open," she says, laughing in place of good-bye.

"What the hell? You were gone forever! I almost hung up," Abby says, not even trying to hide her annoyance.

For a second I think about telling her; it would be good to get a second opinion. But just as quickly, I'm over it. "Sorry," I say.

"Omigod, was it Parker?" she asks, her voice free of anger and now taking on a lower, more gossipy tone. "Is he begging you to come back?"

"Hardly," I say, my mind still reeling with thoughts of Teresa and Marc and what they could possibly have in common. "From what you said, it sounds like he's already moved on."

"So who was it? I waited for over an hour. I deserve to know."

"You're totally exaggerating, but it's not like it's a secret.

It was Teresa. She wants me to stop by," I say, heeding the number one rule about lying (well, maybe number two, after don't get caught) and how it's always safer not to stray too far from the truth.

"Don't do it!" Abby says, sounding completely ominous. "I'm totally serious, do *not* go over there."

"Why?" I ask, striving for blasé, but nailing panic.

"You should've seen the place when we left, I bet it's totally trashed by now. She probably wants you to help clean up. You know, payback for cutting out early."

I close my eyes and sigh in relief, glad that Abby's still unaware of at least some of my secrets. "Okay, listen, I should go," I tell her. "It's getting late, and I haven't even showered yet." I gaze into the mirror and scowl at my limp, boring hair.

"No, you can't go until you answer my question. Should I give Jax a second chance or not?"

I drop back onto my bed, grab two pillows, and prop them under my head. "I don't know, Ab. I mean, do you want to give him another shot?"

"That's why I called you, to help me sort that out."

"Well, what does Jenay say?"

"Jenay? Forget Jenay. I mean, I love her, we all love her, but between you and me, Jenay is now a pep club member. She also believes in pixie dust, pots of gold, unicorns, four-leaf clovers, guardian angels, and leprechauns. She thinks Mickey Mouse is a real person. That's why I called you. Because you're my only levelheaded friend."

I take a deep breath and close my eyes. "Then forget it," I tell her. "It's either there or it's not. And it shouldn't take GPS to locate it."

She sighs. "That's exactly what I was thinking." And then before she hangs up she goes, "Oh hey, what's that song you were humming under your breath?"

I sit up suddenly, my knuckles going white as my fingers grip the phone.

"You know, the one that's all da da dee, do da, da la la la? What is that? It's so haunting."

I listen to her rendition of the song I fell asleep to last night, totally unaware that I'd been humming it that whole time. "Um, I don't even know the name. I think I heard it somewhere on the radio, or maybe I dreamt it or something," I say, laughing nervously, hoping she'll believe me.

"Okay, well, gotta run," she says. "But I'm serious about avoiding Teresa's. If I were you I'd stay away."

Twenty-three

By the time I get to Teresa's, I know I'm too late. And it's not like it took me all that long to shower and dress, it was more the pacing, the hand wringing, and the pro-and-con-list making that ate up all my free time.

There's an old beat-up motorcycle leaning precariously on its kickstand, and one of those jacked-up, overaccessorized, overcompensating, fully loaded trucks parked right beside it. But no blue Camaro. And since neither of those vehicles looks remotely like anything Teresa or her parents would be willing to drive, I'm feeling more than a little anxious.

I hesitate at the door, thinking I should just forget about knocking, cut my losses, and head home. And just as I turn to do exactly that, the front door swings open as Teresa smiles and says, "I saw you from the living room window." Then she wiggles her fingers, motioning me inside.

She leads me past the formal dining room, which looks no

worse for the wear, and through the ultramodern kitchen that's shiny, clean, and pristine. And even though the house is showing absolutely no sings of a wild night of out-of-control teenage debauchery, Teresa's tight ripped jeans and tiny black tube top are giving off a whole other vibe.

So by the time we get to the den and I see those two over-age delinquents sprawled across the couch, let's just say I'm not the least bit surprised.

"You remember Tom and Jason?" she says, nodding at the losers I'd met that day in the park.

I just look at them, wondering why she lured me here, but determined not to show any fear.

"Beer?" she asks, raising a sweaty bottle in offering. Martha Stewart, look out.

But I just shake my head and drop onto an overstuffed chair, doing my best to ignore asshole Tom who, once again, seems dead set on staring at me.

"So, did you go to her little high school soiree?" Tom asks, tilting his head back as he guzzles his beer, his eyes still fixed on mine.

But before I can answer Teresa smiles and goes, "She stopped by, but she didn't stay long."

"Hot date?" he asks, lighting up a cigarette that Jason immediately grabs and breaks in half.

"No smoking in the palace, asshole," Jason says, taking the broken pieces and shoving them into his beer before chucking Tom hard on the back of his head.

I watch as Tom makes a face but still cowers away, and I feel like I'm in one of those weird art-school films. The kind filled with rain, symbolism, and dream sequences that you can't understand. I mean, on the surface, Teresa's probably one of the luckiest people I know. It's like she's living the teenage dream. She's got two parents who are still together, she lives in a beautiful, huge home, she has a walk in-closet that's jammed full of super-cute, designer-label clothes, she's pretty, she's popular, she gets good grades, and she's had the same boyfriend since the end of eighth grade who everyone unanimously agrees is totally hot. Heck, she even has real-deal Hollywood credentials, having starred in a baby-food commercial back when she was two, followed by some small, mostly nonspeaking roles over the last few years. Which also makes her one of the few people who can actually list on her Web page "model, singer, actress," and only the singer part is a lie.

So I don't get it. I mean, why would someone who has all of *that* want to hang out with a cheesy, creepy drug dealer and his mentally challenged sidekick? It just doesn't make any sense.

When I look up, Tom is still staring at me, which totally gives me the creeps, so I pretend I have to go to the bathroom, since it's the only place where I can be alone, clear my head, and hopefully figure out what to do next.

I'm standing in front of the sink, watching the water run down the drain, when Teresa barges in without even knocking. "He just got here," she says, standing in the doorway, looking at me. "I just let him in; I thought you should know. You know, so you don't stay in here all day, wasting water." She smiles, but it's not at all normal. In fact, it's not even kind.

"What's going on?" I ask. "Why'd you invite me here?"

"From what I saw in the park, it seems like you and Marc are really hitting it off," she says, looking right at me. "So I thought you might want to hang in a more private place, with people you can trust."

I just stand there, not saying a word. I mean, I can't exactly deny what she saw. But still, I know better than to trust her.

"I know what you're thinking," she says, nodding her head. "But you've got it all wrong. I'm actually a much better friend than you think. Like last night? After you left? Parker got all hammered and started hitting on someone's girlfriend. They almost got in a fight. But I just calmed everyone down, then I took him aside for a little chat. And you know what he asked? He wanted to know if you were into someone else. He said whenever you guys were alone together, it was like you were never really there."

I look at her, holding my breath.

"But I just told him to go home, sober up, and sleep it off." She shrugs. "So you see, we're not so different, you and me. We both look one way on the outside, but inside, we're something else. We've got secrets." She smiles.

"Why me?" I ask. "I mean, out of all the people you know, why do you share this stuff with me?"

"Because you're smart, and you're different, and you're one of the few people who get how nothing's ever what it seems."

We just stand there, looking at each other, and I wonder if it's really that simple, if even part of that is true. Then she grabs my hand and pulls me toward the door. "Let's go," she says. "Marc doesn't even know you're here."

I follow her out of the bathroom and into the den, where Marc is sitting on a chair, clutching a beer and looking uneasy.

"Look who's here," Teresa says, motioning to me like a game-show model presenting a shiny, new, energy-efficient appliance.

I slip onto a chair and try to act casual, like I hang out with drug dealers and dropouts all the time.

Marc glances at me then over at Jason. Then he sets down his beer and goes, "Listen, can we make this quick? I need to get out of here."

But Jason's taking it easy and refuses to be rushed. "Relax," he says. "Just chill and finish your drink."

I glance at Marc's bottle, seeing how it's still completely full, and remember how he rarely drinks, probably because of his mom's bad habit. "Sorry bro, but I really need to split," he says, like he's speaking a foreign language now, Jason's language.

But Jason just glares, his eyes becoming angry, narrow slits. "Apparently you didn't hear me. I'm. Finishing. My. Beer," he says, his voice firm and controlled, punctuating each separate word.

So we all just sit there. Avoiding each other's gaze while listening to Jason slurp and sip, until he finally finishes it off with one long, loud, disgusting belch. Then he sets his bottle hard on the table and says, "Me and my boy will be right back." He points at all of us, his index finger outstretched, his thumb arched up high, like a gun about to go off. When he pulls the trigger he laughs, as he ushers Marc out of the room.

It feels like forever. Seriously, from the time they leave 'til the moment they come back, it feels like my whole, entire life has passed.

And when Marc finally comes back into the den, he takes one look at me and goes, "Need a ride?"

And I grab my purse and head for the door, without once looking back.

Twenty-four

The second we get in the car, Marc shakes his head and says, "What the hell were you doing in there? Are those people your friends?"

"You know they're not my friends," I say, folding my arms across my chest and staring out the window. I mean, I don't like the tone of his voice. And I don't like the way he's acting. Like I'm some little baby that needs to be protected. Okay, yeah, maybe I didn't *love* being in there, and maybe I'm glad he's whisking me away now. But still, even if he hadn't shown, I totally would've made it out of there. Eventually.

"What were you even doing there in the first place?" he asks, his eyes shielded from me as he stares at the road.

"Teresa invited me." I shrug, deciding to leave it at that. I mean, the fact that I went there for him is clearly none of his business.

"Well, that's just great." He glances over at me and shakes

his head again. "Do you and Teresa even know who those guys are? Do you even know what you're getting yourselves into?"

"Well, you seem to be all filled in, so why don't you tell me?" I say, turning toward him.

But he just stares straight ahead, clenching his jaw as he drives. And when he stops at a light, he goes, "Look, I'm sorry. I'm not trying to sound like your dad or anything. It's just those guys are really bad news and you shouldn't be hanging around them. You shouldn't be anywhere near them."

"You were hanging around them."

"That's different," he mumbles, speeding again now that the light's turned green.

"Yeah? How? Exactly how is it different?"

He looks at me for a moment, then he shakes his head and stares back at the road. "It just is, okay?"

"Why?" I say, unwilling to let it go.

"Echo, Christ, just trust me on this one." He rolls his eyes and checks his side mirror.

I turn in my seat, my eyes traveling over him until coming to rest on his jacket. "I want to see what's in your pocket," I say.

"What?" He looks at me, his eyes wide.

"Show me what's in your pocket. And then I'll decide if I'll trust you."

He takes a deep breath and looks away, but his expression is worried.

"Before you left the room with Jason your pocket was flat and empty. And now it's not. Now it's all bulky like you've got something in it. And I want to know what it is."

"No."

I stare at him, my breath caught in my throat since I wasn't expecting to hear that. I mean, I admit at first I was partly just fooling around, but now that I know he's hiding something, I'm determined to know what it is. "Show me," I say, reaching toward him.

But he takes his hand off the wheel and holds me back against my seat, all the while refusing to look at me.

I stare at him in shock, wondering what he could possibly be hiding. "Then just take me home," I finally say, my voice sounding high pitched and fragile.

"Echo, please." He sighs.

"Now. Take me home right now!" I glare at him, my stomach jumping all around, doing the panic dance.

He looks at me and shakes his head, then he pulls an illegal U-turn and heads toward my home.

But by the time he gets to the end of my street I've changed my mind. I mean, maybe he is only trying to help me, and protect me, and save me in the way he couldn't with Zoë. And acting like this, so ridiculous and immature, only proves how much I need that. Besides, I think it's pretty obvious that there's no need for me to fear him. He's never done anything to hurt me, and he never hurt my sister, and whatever he's got in his pocket is clearly none of my business. "I'm sorry," I say, reaching toward him, hoping he won't push me away like before.

"Forget it," he says, smoothing his long fingers back and forth over the steering wheel while staring straight ahead.

"I guess I was just mad because—"

"No need to explain," he says, still not looking at me.

"I just, I don't like it when you treat me like that. Like I'm some stupid little girl. I mean, I'm all grown up now and you won't even see it." I peek at him, taking in the line of his nose, the strength of his chin, the sweep of his lashes, before looking away.

He takes a deep breath and turns. "Believe me, Echo, I've noticed," he says, his voice sounding thick and resigned.

And without even thinking, I grab his sleeve, pull him close, and kiss him. Softly at first, then harder, more urgent, trying to seal this moment in time, determined to leave an impression.

And after awhile, when he pulls away, he looks into my eyes, cradles my face between the palms of his hands, and says, "Promise me."

I nod, holding my breath, waiting.

"Promise me you'll stay away from Jason."

After dinner, and well after my parents have gone to sleep, I climb out of bed, creep down the hall, and sneak into Zoë's room.

I haven't been in here for over a year. Not since the day the cops showed up with empty hands and hopeless faces. But everything looks exactly the same as it did back then—her blue duvet is still haphazard, having been tossed aside in her usual, early morning rush, and there's a lone white sock still lying on the floor, right next to the rug, where she'd dropped it over a year before.

My mom's the only one who comes in here now, the only one who brushes away cobwebs and handpicks lint from the yellowing sheets. I guess because she couldn't save her daughter in the most important way, she's decided to save her like this. With this freeze-dried room, undisturbed, suspended in time. The perfect contrast to our lives now, which are so completely and irreversibly changed.

I go over to Zoë's dresser and lift her brush, my fingers gliding along the tangle of long dark hairs wrapped tightly around the bristles. Then I reach for her perfume, its cap long ago lost, and bring it to my nose, surprised to find still the faintest hint of scent.

This is where I'd waited while the cops sat downstairs. On the floor, in the middle of her room, right in the center of her crème-colored flokati rug. My eyes shut tight, my body rocking back and forth as my mind sped in reverse, remembering our lives before, refusing to believe how they were about to become.

But when my parents came home, and I heard my mother's long, painful cry, I picked myself up and headed downstairs, knowing it was time to stop pretending.

I move toward Zoë's bed, sit gently on her mattress, and run my hand along her soft, worn sheets. Then I spread my body across the top of her crumpled duvet, molding her soft abandoned pillow against my cheek as I close my eyes, yearning to tell her how much I miss her, wanting to explain about Marc and me. How living her life and sharing her experiences makes me feel closer, like she never really left.

I lay like this for a while, my eyes shut tight, calling her to me.

But when she doesn't come, I turn off the light and creep back to my room. Knowing I've stolen enough for one day.

Twenty-five

July 19

Okay, I'm totally short on time, but I just really need to write about how completely psyched I am that I'm going to Marc's tonight!! Yay! It's finally happening! In fact he's picking me up any second, and I really hope my outfit's okay. I mean, I've seen pictures of his mom and she always looks so polished and expensive. And I just really really want her to like me.

Anyway, it almost didn't happen since my parents were insisting that I stay home to watch Echo—which is so freaking ridiculous I can't even tell you. I mean, hello? Has anyone noticed she's 13 now? I mean, jeez, enough with the overprotective BS, she's a teenager now for G's sake!

But luckily Echo was pretty pissed too, so she told them they were making her feel like a needy little baby. Then after proving she knew how to dial 911 and perform the Heimlich maneuver on herself in case she choked on an Oreo or something, they finally, reluctantly, gave in.

Okay, Marc's here—gotta go!

Oh, never mind. It's just Abby and Jenay. Guess they're having a sleepover or something. Anyway, I'm wearing my favorite cobalt blue dress because I think it looks dressy—but not too dressy. You know, cuz I don't want to look like I'm trying too hard. Because according to Vogue magazine, trying too hard (or at least looking like you're trying too hard) is like fashion sin numero uno. And since his mom can actually afford to buy the clothes they show in Vogue, I figure she could spot a striver over a mile away.

Okay, this time it really is Marc, so I'm outta here! But first, let me just say—

No matter how bad Marc thinks tonight is going to be—I'm totally psyched to be going!!!!

Yay!

July 19
Should have known better. I always get way too excited for my own good. Too tired and sad to write, though, so more later.

July 21
Yesterday was the first time Marc and I went an entire day without speaking to each other. And what made it even worse is the fact that it was a Sunday, which is always our day to hang in the park and feed our adopted pet ducks, or whatever.

But I did try calling him. Only he didn't answer. And for once, I didn't leave a message. I mean, why should I? All he had to do is check the display to know that it was me. Besides, I really didn't know what to say.

He did warn me, though. I'll give him that.

But I guess I just got so excited about seeing the house and meeting his mom that I ignored all the rest. You'd think I would've known better, though. I mean, seriously.

Anyway, when we first got there his mom wasn't home, which made him happy and me disappointed. Not that I wanted to have a whole big thing with her, but still, I'd purposely sat all stiff and careful in the car so I wouldn't get all smudged up or wrinkled and so I'd look great when we got there. Since for the whole entire day I'd imagined the moment when she'd greet us at the door, welcoming me into her home with a big smile and a hug. Okay, so maybe I did kind of want a big thing. But it's not like it matters, since that's not how it turned out.

So Marc gave me a tour of the house and property, and it's so freaking big, I don't know how he finds his way around. Seriously, it's like one of those mansions you see in a magazine or on TV or something. Then afterward, he led me out to the guesthouse (which believe me, is pretty much the size of a normal house) and when I asked, "Who lives here?" he said, "No one. But senior year, it's mine. That's our deal."

"Seriously?" I asked, looking all around, trying to imagine having a sweet setup like that. To just be able to come and go as you please, without having to climb down a tree or creep down the hall, or something.

But he just shrugged like it was no big deal. But I guess rich, privileged people are just used to having sweet deals like that.

Anyway, so then of course he got all handsy and tried to get me to have sex. But no way was I going to get all messed up before I even had a chance to make a good impression on his mom. So after pushing him off like a gazillion times, we just sat on the couch, side by side, watching some dumb show on TV, while he kept groping at me, trying to get me to change my mind. Which I gotta admit, totally got on my nerves.

Then finally, after like the sixth time I thought I heard a car on the drive, there really was a car on the drive, and he looked at me and said, "Cruella's home."

And I go, "You call your mom Cruella?"

But he just laughed and led me back to the house.

"Mother," he said, leaning in for the air cheek kiss just like you see rich people do in movies. "This is Zoë."

She looked at me, her eyes starting at my shoes and working their way up to my forehead.

She's tall, thin, and blond, just like she appears in all those society-page pictures. Only in person, she's really blond. Like Texas blond, almost stripper blond. And when her eyes met mine they narrowed, and suddenly her face went from faded beauty to mean. And believe me, the artist who painted her portrait that hangs in the stairwell failed to capture that.

"Well aren't you a beauty," she said.

And even though that might sound like a compliment to those who weren't around to witness it, trust me, it wasn't. Her voice was hard, her eyes were slits, and her lips were pursed, which are pretty much all the signs for hate at first sight.

"Where'd you find this one?" she asked, glancing at Marc as her heavily ringed fingers sorted through the stack of mail.

I just stood there feeling small and stupid and wishing I'd just listened to Marc when he warned me, wishing I hadn't pushed him so much.

"We go to school together," he said.

"Is that right?" She looked at me again, up once, down once. Then her eyes flicked away, and I knew I'd just been discarded. "Has William returned?" she asked.

Marc said no.

"We'll start without him then. I'm going upstairs to change. Tell Celia to bring me my drink."

Dinner was a nightmare. Going from bad to worse with each passing drink. Things improved slightly when William (stepdad #3) came home, but only because that gave her a new target.

I feel sorry for Marc. I mean, before his mom got home, it all looked so amazing and glamorous. I mean, with the grand staircase, the marble floors, the guesthouse, and the infinity pool. I was actually feeling a little bit jealous, and also kind of judging him for not appreciating it more. But the second she came home, the whole picture changed. And by the time it was over, I just wanted to go home.

But the worst part is, it doesn't make me feel closer to Marc, like I want to help him get through it or anything.

It actually makes me want to run away.

July 29

Marc and I just went almost ten days without seeing each other, and I can still hardly believe it. I mean, it's not like we actually broke up or anything, since we talked on the phone and stuff. I guess it's more like things got so intense so fast that we both feel we need a little cool down. Or at least I do. I'm not really sure how he feels about it, since it's not like anything was ever actually said.

I mean, after that awful dinner, well, I guess I just started thinking about how I've ditched all my friends, and it made me feel bad. It's like, just because Marc likes being a loner doesn't mean I do too. So basically I just spent the last ten days working during the day and hanging with Carly and Paula at night.

At first they gave me a bunch of shit for ditching them like that. But then after, it was like we'd been hanging out the whole entire summer and I'd never really left. I didn't say anything about meeting Marc's mom though. I mean, of course they asked if I'd been to the house and stuff, cuz pretty much everyone always wants to know about that. And since I didn't want to lie I said yes. But then I pretty much left it at that, and any details I did give were totally vague.

Anyway, hanging with them just made me realize how much I missed them. It also made me realize how I'm way too young to keep getting so tied down all the time. I mean, don't get me wrong, I still totally and completely love Marc. But sometimes I just need to hang out and have a little fun with my friends.

August 5
All day yesterday I was at Carly's, setting up my very own page on this Web site where you post pictures of yourself, list all of your favorite things like bands, movies, etc., and try to collect as many friends as possible so you can feel all popular and famous or whatever. And since Carly's been on there for practically ever, she's been bugging me this whole entire time to get on there too, so I finally gave in.

At first it seemed kind of dumb since I can just call her on her cell if I need to leave a message or even send a picture. But then she goes, "What if my ringer's off?"

So I said, "Then I'll text you."

And she went, "Forget it. You have no idea how much better this is, because then everyone can see what you write and what you're doing and saying and stuff."

Which, to be honest, also sounded pretty lame. I mean, I know it's probably old fashioned to even write in a journal when the rest of the world is blogging. But maybe I don't want all these strangers to know what I'm thinking, saying, and doing, you know?

But then she said, "Uh, hello? What do you think it's gonna be like when you're famous? I mean, you think Jessica Simpson gets any privacy?"

She had a point.

Then she goes, "You always talk about how you want to be a model, or actress, or whatever, but if you're that attached to your privacy then maybe you should find a new dream."

So, long story short, I signed on, decorated my space, uploaded some photos, and even though it practically took all day, now I totally get it. Now I totally get what she's been talking about because it's so completely addicting! It's like, within seconds of uploading my first few photos I had like a hundred people asking to be my friend! Okay, maybe most of them were guys, but whatever. And the thing is, all I used are these three stupid little cell phone photos that Paula snapped of me one day when I was laying by her pool.

In one, I'm in my white bikini and I'm laying on the lounger, drinking a beer. In another I'm pretty much doing the same thing, only smiling. And in the third I'm standing up and smiling with my top off. (But only because I didn't want strap marks, and my hands are strategically placed so it's not like you can see anything.)

And I'm thinking, Jeez, if I get all this attention just from these cheesy little cell phone photos, who knows what could happen if I posted some really good, like really professional photos there. You know something sophisticated and classy but a little bit sexy, and yet still kind of innocent too. Since Carly says that all the big New York and L.A. agents are always trolling around on there, scoping for fresh, new faces.

*I'm not sure how she actually knows all that, but still,
it sounds very, very likely.*

*But then she also said that I probably shouldn't tell
Marc because he'll definitely totally freak.*

*And even though I just rolled my eyes and refused to
comment, I'm actually thinking she's right.*

When I close Zoë's diary I feel a little sick. Though I know I
have no one to blame but myself. I mean, it's not like I haven't
already lived through all this. So I shouldn't be surprised
where it leads.

I shove it back under my mattress, finished with it for
now, not willing to claim it in any way.

But at least I know that Marc didn't lie. Not to my parents, and not to the police. He'd stuck by his story the entire
time, never once wavering, even though his alibi has always
been shaky.

He said he was waiting at the park, down by the lake,
where they always used to sit. That he just hung out, doing his
homework, and waiting 'til well after dark. But when she
didn't come back, he tried calling her cell a bunch of times,
only she never answered. And since her phone was never recov-
ered, it took a few days for the cops to confirm that.

"Still," they said. "You could've stood right there, over the
body, making those calls. You know, to cover. Because you
panicked. Because you saw what you'd done to her, saw her lying there like that, and you freaked. Come on, you can tell us.
We're here to help you. So the sooner you confess, the better."

Marc refused a lawyer, refused to change his story. He just
handed over her backpack and said the only reason he even had
it was because she'd left it with him as proof she'd return.

It's weird how the police uncovered her life a lot quicker
than her body. How within just a few days they knew most all
of her secrets—about the Web page, the photo shoot, and her

increasingly volatile relationship with Marc. They even interviewed her friends—Carly, Paula, practically everyone she knew. And believe me, they were all too eager to spill the beans on some things, while completely clamming up on others. But the one thing they all had in common is that every one of them pointed the finger at Marc. Saying how they were always suspicious of his loner ways and his completely messed up family.

"He isolated Zoë."

"He kept her all to himself and totally freaked when she tried to pull away."

But none of it's true. None of it matches anything I've read.

And you'd think that Carly, of all people, would've been above that. Especially since she was Zoë's best friend. But the truth is, it took her awhile to finally give them the more important details, and I always wondered who she was trying to protect—Zoë or herself?

I mean, she's the one who pushed it. She's the one who encouraged her to go. Not that I think it's her fault or anything, because clearly it was Zoë's choice in the end. Though I guess it explains why she tries so hard to avoid me at school, and how she can barely manage to look me in the eye when we pass in the halls.

And yeah, so maybe Marc is kind of a loner. I mean, so what? That doesn't prove anything. That doesn't make him guilty of anything other than having the rare ability to be comfortable just being by himself. Not to mention that it's that *exact* quality, aside from his sexy good looks, that attracted Zoë to him in the first place. It's what made her want him even more.

Though I do know that he hated all of that modeling stuff, and Zoë's celebrity ambitions. He thought that whole world was sleazy and shallow and awful. That it took naïve hungry people and built them way up before spitting them right out again. So it's probably true that he would've freaked if he'd known about those pictures. But that's why Zoë kept it hidden. And by the time he found out, it was already too late.

It took six long months to catch the guy who did it. But only because he tried to do it again. He lured the victim to the exact same location using the exact same M.O. And just like with Zoë, instead of packing a camera, he brought a knife.

He left a six-inch scar across that poor girl's neck. But hey, at least she got to keep her head. My sister wasn't so lucky.

And it was *that,* they said, that finally took her.

And even though they caught him red-handed (trust me, no pun intended), not one thing changed for Marc. And those six months he spent as a suspect may as well have been a conviction. I mean, maybe he didn't go to prison for a crime he didn't commit. But then again, he didn't have to.

Our town became his jailer.

Twenty-six

At first I was worried how Parker would act. Would he be angry, dismissive, sad, happy, euphoric, grateful?

But then I decided not to care.

And it's not because I was the least bit proud of the way I'd handled things. To be honest, I wasn't proud of much of anything I'd done. It was more like now that it was over, I was over it too.

Though I was determined to deal with Teresa. I mean, I still had no idea what her motive might be, not to mention why she insisted on even hanging with me in the first place. And I needed her to know, once and for all, that she was wrong about me, that no matter what she thought, she and I were totally different, we had nothing in common, we were nothing alike. And that any secrets I may have had, I was now more than willing to blow right open.

So right before lunch I stand by her locker, just waiting for her to show. And when she sees me she waves and smiles and says, "Hey! Let me just dump these books and we'll head on over."

But I just look her right in the eye and recite the speech I'd been rehearsing all day in my head. "I'm not eating at the table," I say. "I'm hanging with Marc. And just so you know, I don't care who you tell, or what you say, because I'm all out of secrets. But don't forget, I still have yours." Then before she can even respond, I turn and walk away, heading over to where Marc sits, feeling the weight of her stare the entire way.

It feels good to have nothing to hide. To no longer care what everyone thinks. Because knowing the real truth makes nothing else matter. And the real truth is that the only thing Marc has ever been guilty of is loving my sister. Despite what these small-minded people still say.

Because the fact is, Zoë never told him! I read it for myself. And if he didn't know what she was up to, then how was he supposed to stop her? How could he possibly have done anything to save her?

And even though I feel pretty awful to admit it, I really need a break from Abby and Jenay. I mean, I love them, don't get me wrong. And the last thing I'd ever want is for them to feel hurt or abandoned by me. But all the stuff they're into now, everything they care about, is just so standard-issue teen—so normal and typical and boring and mundane, like they're living in a sitcom, instead of the real world like me.

And it's not that I don't wish I could live like that too, because I really truly do. But unfortunately, that's no longer an option. And no matter how much I might want for things to be different, there are some things I just can't change. I mean, they don't know what it's like to live under the shadow of a sister like Zoë. They don't know what it is to live with a vacant, numb, pill-popping mom and an absentee dad, and to have the whole town point and whisper whenever you go by. They'll never know the pain of hearing the exact same people who left angels and cards for my sister's memorial, gossiping behind her back, slandering her character, and acting like she somehow deserved it.

But I do know what it's like to live like that. And that's why I'll never be able to blend. I'll never be able to care about pep club or which jeans to wear to a party or who will ask me to a dance.

I'm a freak. There's just no getting around it. And even though it wasn't by choice, now that it's a fact I have to find a way to live with it. And hanging with Abby and Jenay and all of their "normalness" only emphasizes my "weirdness." So I need to find a place where I won't always feel so strange and obtrusive. I need to be with someone who's a lot more like me.

"Hey," I say, sliding onto the bench next to Marc and tapping him on the shoulder, since he's wearing earphones with his eyes closed, which means he can't hear or see me.

He opens his eyes and smiles, then scoots over to give me more space.

And when he removes his earpiece I say, "Is it okay if I sit here with you?" I tear into a bag of chips, then thrust it toward him, offering him first pick.

"What about your friends?" he asks, looking at me intently, his deep dark eyes traveling over my face.

But I just shrug. "I thought you were my friend."

He looks at me for a moment, then nods and inserts his earpiece.

And I eat my lunch while he listens to music. And even though it may look strange on the outside, on the inside, where it really counts, I'm finally at peace.

Abby and Jenay were so freaked about lunch, the whole way home it's pretty much all they talk about.

"I just don't get it," Abby says, while Jenay nods in agreement.

"There's nothing to get," I tell them, trying to maintain my calm, yet feeling completely annoyed at having to defend myself.

Abby shakes her head. "Um, actually there's plenty to get. Like your sister for instance? Not to mention what everyone's saying." They both look at me.

Before I respond, I take a deep breath, reminding myself not to get angry, that they're my best friends and they only want what's best for me.

But it doesn't work, so I shake my head and say, "I'm only going to say this once so I hope you both listen. Marc is in no way, shape, or form, the least bit responsible for what happened to Zoë." I look at them. "And if you guys think you or anyone else in this town knows more about it than I do, well, you're wrong. Because I'm the only one in this school, the only one in this whole entire *town*—outside of the cops and my parents—who knows *all* of the facts and details. And believe me, sometimes I wish I didn't, but I do, and there's nothing I can do about it. I'm also well aware of what all these small-minded idiots are saying, and how ninety-nine percent of it's lies." I shake my head and fold my arms across my chest. "But the worst part is knowing that half the people responsible for those lies used to be Zoë's friends. So I'm hoping you guys can do a little better. I'm hoping you can be a better friend to *me* than they were to *her*, and try not to judge me or second-guess me, because I just might know something you don't."

By the time I'm finished I'm totally shaking, and my friends just stand there, eyes wide, mouths open, not saying a word. And feeling kind of embarrassed for going off like that and not knowing how to recover, I just turn away and head toward home.

Later that night Teresa calls. But when I see her number on the display I completely ignore it. And then right before I've almost fallen asleep, it rings again. Only this time it's Marc.

"I'm outside. Wanna go for a ride?" he offers.

And after throwing on some jeans, boots, and my favorite sweater, I brush my hair, swipe on some lip gloss, spritz some perfume, open the french doors, shimmy down the tree, and run across the wet frosted grass toward his car.

As he navigates the dark quiet streets, I wonder if we're going to the park. But when he brakes at the top of old Water Tower Hill, all I can do is laugh.

"You're joking, right? The water tower?" I say, shaking my head. "I mean, if you've really got your own guesthouse all to yourself, then why are you bringing me here?"

During the day Water Tower Hill is known as the local eyesore. But at night, it's known as the local underage make out place—where teens from as far as three towns over come to park, drink, smoke, and hook up. It even has its own creepy legend that seems to attract more people than it scares away.

Rumor has it that a long time ago, like back in the seventies or something, some girl from the next town over came here to cheat on her boyfriend. But evidently he was on to her, because he followed her here, parked far away, then crept toward her car. When he peeked in through the window and saw her and her lover kissing, he freaked out so bad he reached for his gun, pressed the barrel against the glass, and pulled the trigger twice, one shot for each head.

Apparently the impact of the blast tore them apart, leaving one hanging half out the window, and the other slumped over the seat. And it wasn't until he opened the door and the lover fell out that he realized he was a she.

So now the story goes that the two slain lovers both haunt the place, protecting all the young innocent girls from men with bad intent.

And when I gaze at Marc I wonder about his intent, because I know I'm innocent, though maybe not for long.

Besides, it's not like I'd ever actually believe a story like that.

Because ghosts are only real if you don't really miss someone. When you do, they're just a cruel joke.

"It's beautiful up here. Just look at the lights," he says, the leather of his jacket squeaking as he rolls the window down just a crack.

"Yeah, the only time this town ever looks good is when you're looking down on it," I say, wondering if Zoë's looking down on us, and if so, what it is that she's thinking.

He kisses me then, as I knew he would. I mean, why even come here, if you're not gonna try?

My fingers are tangled in his hair, the pads of my thumbs smoothing those glorious, high cheekbones, as my mouth moves hungrily against his, wanting to capture this moment, willing it to never end.

"Zoë," he whispers, lifting my sweater as his hands search for my breasts.

I lean in, kissing him even harder, feeling his fingers fumbling with the clasp at my back. "Here, let me help you," I say, reaching behind.

But then he pushes me away, until I'm back in my seat, his face a horrified mask when he realizes what he just said.

But I don't mind. In fact, I prefer it. So I lean toward him again, my mouth seeking his, but settling for his cheek. "Don't worry," I say, my lips grazing against the coarse black stubble that grows along his jaw. "It's okay, really. I like being her."

But he shakes his head and pushes me off, dropping his head in his hands as he says, "Oh God, Echo. Oh my God, what have I done?" He hides his face in shame, as he trembles and shakes, mumbling a whole string of words I can't understand.

I just sit there, wanting to comfort him, desperately wanting to rewind and pick up right where we left off. But then he wipes his face with his sleeve, reaches for the key and turns it hard, startling the engine back to life. "I'm taking you home," he says, staring straight ahead, no longer willing to look at me.

But I just fold my arms across my chest and glare at him, refusing to be discarded, refusing to let go of the best thing that ever happened to me. "No," I say, my eyes narrowed, my mouth set.

He rubs his eyes and shakes his head, and suddenly he looks so much older and so incredibly tired. "I'm taking you home, Echo. We're leaving, now. So please fix your top, so we can get out of here."

I sit there, staring out the window, my lips trembling as though I might cry. Doesn't he realize how much I need to be here? Doesn't he realize how I'd much rather be Zoë than me?

But he just looks at me for the longest time, then he rubs his eyes again and says, "Don't you get it? I've done enough damage. I can't go hurting you too." His jaw is quivering, his eyes black and hard, and he looks like he's on the verge of something he can barely contain.

And when I realize his words I feel a chill down my spine. So I straighten my sweater, hug my knees to my chest, and stay like that the entire way.

Twenty-seven

When he stops at the corner, I throw the door open and hit the ground running. Sprinting across the frozen lawn with my shoes still in hand, my toes turning blue, my breath coming fast and quick, 'til I finally reach my room where I grab Zoë's diary and flop on the bed, desperate for answers, and knowing she's the only one who can provide them, the only one who can explain what Marc really meant when he said, "I can't go hurting you too."

> *August 7*
>
> *Only three more days 'til Dr. Freud goes on vacation! Which means only three more days 'til I go on vacation too! But it's not like we're going together (gag). It's just that there's no work for me to do when he's gone.*
>
> *Anyway, I can't freaking wait! I feel like I'm finally getting my summer back. And all I plan to do for those three*

blissful weeks is sleep, hang out with Paula during the day, and Marc every night.

We've been getting along so much better over the last few days, which makes me feel really bad about freaking out like that over his mom and stuff. I mean, it's not like he actually dragged me there, or even wanted me to go. It's more like I pushed and pushed 'til he finally gave up and gave in. And because of that, now I have to live with the consequences, along with the memory of her nasty little "Where'd you find this one?" comment. Like I'm just one more slut he dragged home.

Marc swears that's just her typical passive-aggressive game. So I looked that up in one of Dr. Freud's books, and it seems like the right diagnosis to me. He also said she's all freaked out about getting old, and about her fading looks and saggy chin (okay, he didn't really say that part about her chin, that was pure me!), so she pretty much hates anyone younger and prettier than her. Which is basically like half the population, but whatever.

So, Carly keeps begging me to go meet this guy she's been messaging back and forth on her Web page. But I'm like, "No freaking way. Forget it. Not to mention, hello, what about Stephen?"

And she goes, "I am so over Stephen! Why didn't you warn me about that bicep gazing bullshit?"

And I go, "Believe me, I did."

Anyway at first I said a definite no. But then, by the time I left I changed it to maybe. But I told her not to tell him I was coming too, because then he might get the wrong idea and try to bring a friend. And not only am I not going to cheat on Marc, but it will be a lot safer if it's two against one. I mean, just in case it comes to that.

So she goes, "What do you see in him anyway? I

mean, besides the gorgeous, hot, bad boy sexy stuff. Is it the money?"

But I just shrugged. Because even though she finally figured out the whole ugly truth about Stephen, that doesn't mean she can even begin to understand a guy like Marc. So I go, "He's just different from everyone else. He's not one size fits all."

And she just shook her head and looked at me and said, "I'll say."

August 8

Okay, so we're meeting Mr. Internet tonight at seven. And I've lied to just about everyone I know to pull it off. My parents think I'm going out with Carly (which I am, just not to where I said we were going), her parents think she's going out with me (ditto), but not a soul knows anything more. Not even Paula knows the truth, cuz I know she'd just totally freak. Actually, they'd all freak.

Though I do feel really bad about lying to Marc and telling him I'm staying home to hang out with Echo for a change. I mean, I know that's actually really really really seriously bad karma, since I've been meaning to spend more time with her, and now I supposedly am, only it's a lie.

But I swear, if this guy turns out to be totally cool and not some Dateline Special Internet predator freak, then I'll take the kid out for shopping and lunch. Really. Scout's honor.

August 9

Okay, so at first Carly and I were totally amazed that the guy turned out to look a lot like his picture, which was actually pretty cute. But what wasn't so amazing is that apparently the picture was taken like, over ten years ago. Because up close and in person he looks a lot more like thirty than twenty like he said on his page.

Anyway, you should've seen his face when he saw Carly and me walking toward him. His eyes went all wide and he got this big grin, like he just won the lottery or something. So we totally hung out and talked for a while, then Carly told him we wanted to party and asked him to go buy us some beer since we're underage and can't score it ourselves.

Well, it was pretty obvious that the whole "underage" bit got him major excited. So the second he returned and set the package down, Carly grabbed the bag and said, "Adios, loser!"

And then we totally took off!

Seriously, we just started walking away, but all casual, not like rushing or anything, which actually made him pretty mad, to say the least. So he yelled at us to come back, but I turned and went, "If you take one more step toward us I'm calling the cops and reporting you for the pervert you know that you are." And I held up my cell phone like I was just about to do it.

You should've seen his face! He just stood there, totally stunned. But still, he totally backed down. He just looked at us all sad and said, "Well, can I at least have the wine back? That's an expensive bottle."

But Carly goes, "No, because you're a pervert! Which means you don't deserve any wine."

Then we took our stash over to Paula's, where we hung in the Jacuzzi, and told her the story over and over, and each time it just got better.

August 10

Today was a short day since Dr. Freud had a flight to catch, so we said aloha then I waited outside for Marc.

Only he didn't show.

So then I called him and went, "Where are you?"

And he said, "Home."

"Well you're supposed to be here," I told him.

But he pretended he didn't know what I was talking about, which is totally ridiculous since I told him twice this morning and even left a message at lunch.

But he just goes, "Didn't get it."

"Well you're getting it now. So hurry up and come get me," I said, my patience running big-time thin.

And then, I still can't believe this, he goes, "I can't."

"What do you mean you can't? I thought you said you were home?" I was completely fuming and no longer trying to hide it. "I mean, it's like a hundred degrees out here and I'm melting," I tell him.

But he just gives me a bunch of bull about how busy he is, which is total crap since it's not like he has a job or chores or anything. And when I asked him just what exactly he was busy with he totally ignored me! He just went, "Sorry, I can't get you, but I'll definitely see you tonight though, okay?"

I felt like throwing my phone at the building I was so mad. But I didn't. Instead, I just sucked it up and went straight to Carly's. And by the time I got there I was still so pissed I ended up telling her the whole ugly story, which is something that I never, ever do. Mostly because once you tell your friends the bad stuff, that's all they seem to remember.

But still, it felt so much better just to get it off my chest. Not to mention how she was totally sympathetic and only a little bit judgmental. And then she grabbed her laptop and tried to find me a new boyfriend on the Internet, which I took as a joke, even though I think she was partly serious.

Then we clicked over to my page so I could upload some more pictures we took of us pretending to French-kiss each other. Then we made fun of all the perverts who messaged me, telling me how I looked totally cool and laid back and asking me if I wanted to maybe hang out and chill— please.

But I still hooked up later with Marc, and even though I was still pretty mad, I decided to just let it go because my vacation just started and I was determined to be happy and have fun. Plus, I hate to stay angry and carry grudges and stuff.

But still, every time I asked him where he was, he just changed the subject and moved on to something else.

I must have fallen asleep, because when I wake up my mom is standing over me and staring down at me. "Echo, are you feeling all right?" she asks, leaning toward me brushing her palm across my forehead, fever sweeping.

Physically, I'm fine. But emotionally, I'm a wreck. All I can think about is Marc, and the words he said right before driving me home. I mean, what exactly happened between my sister and him? And what was he hiding in his pocket that day? So far, I've yet to read a single thing in Zoë's diary that could even begin to explain.

Not to mention how there's no way I can face Abby and Jenay. Not after yesterday's emotional tirade.

So I decide to do something I haven't done since I was hellbent on avoiding the presidential fitness test back in sixth grade—I fake sick.

"I'm feeling kinda lousy," I say, squinting at her as I conjure up images of hot furnaces, burning matches, the scorching desert heat, and the bowels of hell—method acting for raising my temperature.

"What's the matter?" she asks, sliding onto the edge of my bed and readjusting the covers in a way that brings her hand dangerously close to the partially exposed diary.

I shift my body, flopping the covers over it, trying to make it appear as though I'm sickly and distressed, when really I just need to keep that little blue book far out of her reach.

"I'm nauseous," I say, allowing myself a mental high five for the stroke of sudden genius. I mean, that's one that can never be disproved, since it's only felt by its host.

"Anything else?" she asks, her face growing worried and stained with concern.

Jeez, she wants more? What is this? "Um, yeah, I think I also feel a headache coming on, probably nothing major, but then again, it just started. I'm also a little weak, but that's probably just the fatigue," I mumble, rearranging my face to resemble someone who's fighting burgeoning, yet intolerable pain.

"Sounds like the flu. There's a bug going around," she says, smoothing her skirt as she stands. "I'll call the school and tell them you won't be there today."

"Do you think you can call Abby too? And tell her I won't be meeting them on the corner?" I ask, even though I doubt they're expecting me, not after my outburst.

"Of course," my mother says. "But I'm worried about leaving you here all alone, feeling this way."

"Oh, I'll be all right. Really," I say, hoping I haven't gone too far, praying she won't try to use this as an excuse to call in sick too.

Twenty-eight

Remember how I said I like having the house to myself? Well being home alone for the whole entire day is like Heaven. Seriously. And with my mom finally gone and fully convinced that I'm planning a day of bed rest (but that I won't hesitate to call her if necessary), I grab the diary and take it downstairs, where I make myself a nice, healthy (well, kind of) breakfast.

I pour some frosted cereal into a bowl then add more sugar and nonfat (that's the healthy part) milk, then I prop the diary before me and begin reading, trying to get the spoon from the bowl to my mouth without splattering the pages.

August 11
Today is the second official day of my vacation and I really thought it would be nice if I could spend it with my boyfriend but apparently he has other plans. Some big effin secret he refuses to tell me.

And to be honest, I'm really getting sick of it. I mean, it's not like I keep secrets from him, at least not about anything he actually needs to know about. But this is different, this is important. I can just tell.

But you know what? Screw him! I'm just gonna spend the whole day at Paula's, laying by the pool, and not even think about him or his stupid secret. I'm just gonna pretend that he and his little mystery don't even exist.

I know I probably sound like a brat, but it's just that lately, every single passing day is starting to feel exactly the same as the one before it. Like my life is just one long, continuous rerun, with no new episodes scheduled. And it's starting to make me feel really really restless, and more than a little anxious about the future. I mean, I know everything about my life probably seems pretty normal, and not all that bad compared to some, but the thing is, I never wanted to be normal, and I certainly never wanted to be just like everyone else. I've always dreamed of something bigger and better and brighter.

I've always wanted more.

Like, you know how when you watch those teen reality shows on MTV and stuff? And how everyone's always out shopping, or going to parties, or fashion shows, or clubs, or charity events, or whatever, and then how after their turn on the series is over they all get magazine covers, movie deals, recording contracts, product endorsements, and regular spots in the tabloids? When just one year before they were just another kid with a normal life, in a much-better-than-normal town? Well, that kind of stuff makes it so crystal clear just how slow and boring it is here. Not to mention how I'm missing out on some mega opportunities, all because my parents are determined to live in this wasteland—this stupid, boring, totally fucked-up zip code.

I mean, it's not like MTV would ever even consider coming here. So I think it's obvious that if I really want to make something of myself (of my life!), then I'm really left with no choice but to get the hell out of this dead-end town. Seriously. And even though my parents are already starting with the big expectations and college talk (well, as college professors they've actually been at it for years, only now it's more focused and serious), I have to find a way to tell them that their hopes and dreams have nothing in common with mine. And as far as college goes, well, it's just not gonna happen for me.

Because, let's face it, my grades are total sliders—good enough to pass class and not get yelled at too much, but nowhere near their Ivy League standards. And if they think I'm going local, then they're completely loco. I'd never go to the same lame school where my mom and dad teach.

It's like, let Echo go to Harvard, since she's the brainy one who cares about all that intellectual, deep stuff. Let her be the one who makes them proud. I mean, maybe I'm just not smart like that. Maybe I've got other (better) things to do. And going to college just to please them will only end up putting me four years behind.

So lately I've been thinking about graduating early. I figure I can either beef up my credits (not exactly sure how, but I plan to find out), or take my GED and say an early adios. I mean, I've always wanted to be a model/actress—seriously, ever since I was a really little kid that's all I've ever wanted to do. And I just read this article in one of my magazines about some 14-year-old girl who's storming the European runways! Seriously—the chick is only 14! And I'm already 16—and then next year I'll be 17—and it's just gonna keep on going like that! Which means I really can't afford to waste any more time messing around with my friends and waiting for my boyfriend to call.

I've got to start making a plan for escape. So I can ditch this town and go live my dream before it's too late!

I mean, if Carly and Paula want to lay around the pool all day, making dates with perverts in exchange for free beer, before moving on to junior college and husbands and babies and a bin full of smelly diapers and never once being interviewed on Access Hollywood, then that's fine. Whatever makes them happy.

But that kind of mundane life will never be enough for me. So with that in mind, I've decided to put my Web page to better use. I've decided to make it work for me. And no way am I mentioning it to Marc.

Because if he can have a secret, then I can too.

August 12

Went shopping for back-to-school clothes with Mom and Echo, and when Mom refused to buy me the jeans I wanted, I just pulled out a wad of cash and bought them myself. Hah! The power of employment! And seeing her face go all tight and twisted made it totally worth spending all of my hard-earned dough.

"You're the one who wanted me to work," I couldn't help but remind her. "You're the one who found me the high-paying job!"

I swear, I can't wait 'til I'm a model making a gazillion trillion dollars, driving a Mercedes, living in an awesome penthouse apartment chock full of Jimmy Choos and Prada bags, and sending my parents on vacations in exotic locales—just to get them out of my hair! Let's see who judges me then!

After shopping we went for lunch, and just as I stuck my fork in my salad Echo announced that she's already completed her summer reading list and is getting a head start on the books she heard she'll have to read during the school year.

Jeez! Sometimes I can't believe that we're actually sisters. Seriously. I mean, I love her, I really, really do, but sometimes it seems like she's from another planet. Or maybe it's me. Maybe I really am adopted like I used to dream about when I was younger. Because despite having my father's eyes and my mother's nose, there's no way in hell I'm even remotely DNA connected to these people.

Oh yeah, I also got these really awesome shoes, a couple new sweaters, and a really cute fall coat with a fake fur collar (since I would never wear real fur, I love animals too much, and I plan to make sure that's included in all of my modeling contracts).

But it's not like I can actually wear any of it right now since it's still so freaking hot out. But still, maybe I'll just pack it all up and drag it over to Carly's so she can take some photos of me in it. I need some new pictures for my page since I'm planning a complete overhaul. I'm totally gonna delete all the slutty, stupid, bullshit quotes, and any and all comments regarding drinking, sex, or partying. I'm even gonna switch the background wallpaper to something clean, and sleek, and modern. I'm gonna make it like my online portfolio. So it needs to look as professional as possible.

And even though I still haven't told Marc anything about it, last night when we were all at Kevin's, Paula totally let it slip.

"Omigod," she said. "Remember when we put that picture on your site, the one where you had your top off and then all those guys started instant messaging you?"

I just sat there, totally bugging, and thinking how I was going to kill her the second I could get her alone.

But then Carly goes, "That was my site, dummy. Zoë doesn't have a site, remember?"

And then Paula looks at me, and goes, "Oh yeah, duh! Somebody pass me another beer! Ha ha!"

And then everyone laughed, including me because I felt like I had to, to make it look real.

Marc was the only one who didn't laugh. Marc just stared.

August 16

One week down, two to go! Been hanging at Paula's every day, read the first two pages of one of the books from the eleventh-grade summer reading list—boring! Saw Marc every night except for one where he acted all mysterious so I acted like I didn't care.

Still working on the revamp of my new Web page, though I'm still not all that thrilled with the photos Carly took. I mean, right after I uploaded them, I waited for the usual comments to come pouring in, but mostly I just got stuff like:

Bikini pics way hotter!

Girl-on-girl action mo betta!

So I guess that means if I wanted to be a porn star I'd be set. But that's not gonna happen—I mean, disgusting! Not to mention how the only lingerie ads I'd ever be willing to do are for Victoria's Secret. I mean, if it's good enough for Giselle, then it's good enough for me, but otherwise, that kind of stuff is usually sleazy and cheesy.

Anyway, I think it's getting painfully obvious how I definitely need to get some professional pictures taken by a real photographer, in a real studio, as opposed to a bunch of cell phone digitals taken by my drunk, burnout friend in her poorly lit bathroom.

And then, wouldn't you know it, just when I was

actually considering returning those awesome two-hundred-dollar jeans (that I already wore) so I'll have more money to add to the professional photographer savings account I keep stashed under my mattress I get a message from a professional photographer!

Seriously! Apparently he stumbled across my page and saw my photos and thinks I have potential but the pictures are way too amateur! Duh. So he told me to check out his Web page to see some of his work, and to let him know if I'm interested.

So of course I clicked right over and checked out his pictures, which I gotta say are completely amazing! Seriously nice high fashion black-and-whites, along with some really great head shots, some of which feature models that I'm actually familiar with! And I was so majorly excited I was just about to e-mail him back, when Marc called. So instead I just bookmarked the page, figuring it's probably better to wait a few days and not look all desperate and overly eager.

But still—kismet, fate, destiny, providence, big-time amazing luck—call it what you want, it's finally starting to happen for me!

August 18

I'm totally freaked and don't know what to do. And the worst part is I can't tell anyone, at least not until I know what it means, because maybe it won't end up meaning anything. But at the moment, I just can't seem to figure it out. And believe me, I've tried.

Okay, so I was just out with my dad, on our way downtown, and just as we drove past the office where I work I saw Marc opening the door and going inside. And even though I immediately turned around in my seat and did a total double take just to make sure it was him, the whole thing happened so fast I just couldn't be positive.

But I still have to stress how it really, really, really looked like him. I mean, let me put it this way, how many guys in this town are that good looking and just happen to dress in all black and wear Doc Marten boots when it's one hundred and two in the shade?

Only one that I know of.

And it's not like it would be such a big deal, except for the fact of how he told me he was going to be home all day, doing some work on his car. So right after the sighting, I tried to reach him on his cell, but he must've turned it off cuz it went straight into voice mail. Which, okay, fine, maybe he doesn't want to have it on when he's working on his car, I mean, that makes sense, right?

But then here's the thing—the only people who occupy that office are two shrinks. My boss, who I know for a fact is away on vacation, and the other one who's this psychiatrist (which, I recently found out, means he went to school even longer so he can make even more money and prescribe drugs) who doesn't leave for vacation 'til my boss gets back.

And then I remember that comment Mark made that one day about my boss having a goatee, and how it got me all wondering how he would even know that since it's not like they'd ever met or had ever seen each other.

And even though I shrugged it off at the time, now I'm starting to wonder just how many secrets he's actually keeping from me.

Because to be honest, it seems like they're starting to multiply.

August 20

That photographer dude just sent me another message, which seems a little weird and desperate. But then Carly goes, "Well maybe he just wants to be the one who discovers you, because if you become famous, then it's like big-time kudos for him, right?"

And when you think about it, she really does have a point. Anyway, I didn't message him back yet, 'cause I'm meeting Carly soon and I need to concentrate on that right now. I mean, I finally broke down and told her all about how I saw Marc at the shrink's office and how weird things have been with us lately.

And then she was all, "What's that about?"

And I'm like, "Who knows?"

Then she says, "Well, don't you have a key?"

And I go, "Yeah, but it's only to the front door and his office. Not the other guy's place."

And she goes, "Well, it's a start."

August 21

Marc just called to make plans for our two-months-since-we-first-kissed anniversary and I don't even know what to say. I mean, just two days ago I would've thought that was extremely romantic, but now it's kind of creeping me out. I guess it's because of what I found out. Or more like what I kind of found out. Because sometimes having only a partial answer is worse than not knowing at all.

August 22

Finally called Marc back (I know, I know, bad girlfriend). Anyway, I told him dinner at Giorgio's tomorrow night sounds good, but that I wouldn't be able to see him 'til then.

But still, the more I think about it, the more I think it's probably nothing, since he's never done anything major to weird me out before (and you'd think I'd know by now if he had psycho tendencies or something). And I've definitely never seen him do anything remotely violent or destructive, and the only time he's ever playing with fire is when we're smoking, which doesn't really count as playing with fire, right? (Just playing with your health—ha ha!) Anyway, I'm actually starting to wonder if maybe I'm the one who's crazy!

I mean, I love him—I really, truly, totally do! And I can hardly believe the way I'm totally overreacting to something that in all likelihood is probably nothing! And I really have to stop acting like this because if I don't then I'm totally going to sabotage the only relationship I've ever had that's actually made me feel extremely happy.

Not to mention how I need to learn to give him some space and respect his privacy since it's really not necessary for two people to know absolutely everything about each other. In fact, it's better not to. At least that's what they say in Cosmo.

But still, I just can't stop wondering why Marc wouldn't tell me that he's seeing a shrink. Unless it's because I always make fun of my boss and the psychos who see him, in which case, I feel even worse.

August 23

Today I went shopping, thinking I'd buy something new and exciting to wear to my anniversary dinner tonight with Marc. But since everything that's out now is pretty much for fall, and with the daytime temperatures still in the triple digits—and the nighttime only slightly cooler than that—I decided to just save my money and wear something I already have. Besides, it's not like I'm all that excited about it anyway, not to mention how I need to start saving as much money as possible to invest in my photos, my future, and my one-way ticket out of this hell town.

And then just as I was about to leave, I remembered how Echo's b-day is totally coming up. And since I was already out shopping, I figured I might as well get a head start and buy something early, as opposed to picking up something in a last-minute panic like I usually do.

But since she's not all that into clothes yet, and since she barely wears any makeup or perfume, and since she doesn't seem to focus much on her hair, that pretty much ruled out all of my areas of expertise.

So I headed over to the bookstore, where she likes to spend all her free time, but even though it's not like it was the first time I'd ever gone in there (I mean, I'm not re-tarded, I just don't like to read), still, walking around and trying to choose a book for her was basically impossible. I mean, there's like so many titles, by so many writers, and that's just in the teen section! And knowing Echo, she's probably read every last one of them anyway. And not wanting to give her a repeat, I decided to bail.

Then just as I was on my way out the door, I spotted this display with like, all these book accessories and stuff, which I know probably sounds stupid since it's not like people actually dress up their books like you do a doll, I just mean stuff like fancy jeweled and beaded book-marks and little metal clip-on reading lights and stuff like that. And then just as I was thinking about getting her a bookmark/reading light combo gift set, I noticed this whole other shelf filled with diaries just like the one I'm writing in now!

And I thought, oh my God, that's it! I'll get her a di-ary. I mean, she's going into eighth grade, and that's pretty much when all the big drama starts, right? And it might be nice for her to have something private to record it all in, like when she gets her first crush, or first kiss, or starts fighting with Jenay and Abby, or reads a really exciting sentence in one of her books! (Just kidding about the last one because I *know it sounds mean.) And since she's so into reading and writing and stuff, I figure she'll probably end up writing in her diary even more than I do mine.*

So at first I reached for the cobalt blue one—I guess I'm just naturally drawn to that color—but then I thought how it's probably better if she doesn't have the exact same one as mine. I mean, for starters we're complete and total opposites which means we don't share the same taste in color either, and second, can you imagine if we had the exact same ones and then they somehow got switched!

And since that's the kind of risk I'm just not willing to take, I ended up buying her this really pretty turquoise one. Still blue, only different, calmer, like Echo. And since I still feel so guilty for never taking her to lunch (even after I promised I would if I survived that first Internet hookup meeting thing with Carly—which obviously I did), I bought some really pretty silver wrapping paper (instead of using old Xmas paper like I usually do), a pretty cobalt blue bow (so she'd know at first sight it's from me), and then this little vanilla-scented candle to go with it, so that she can close her door, light her candle, and write about all the amazing things that happen in eighth grade.

And then after I came back home and wrapped it all up, I hid it in the back of my closet, behind my big stack of shoe boxes so she won't find it. I just hope I don't forget that it's there—because you know how it goes, outta sight, outta mind and all that.

I drop the diary and bolt upstairs to Zoë's room, my hands shaking and my heart racing as I dive straight into her closet, pushing aside the tall stacks of shoe boxes, desecrating a space that's been preserved for well over a year.

And sure enough, just like she promised, there's a dark green shopping bag hidden in the back. So I take it over to her bed, where I sit on the edge, anxious to get inside.

But the moment that silver-wrapped box is on my lap, I'm suddenly reluctant to open it. Because this was meant to be unwrapped in a room full of laughter, family, and friends. It was never supposed to happen like this.

Though knowing Zoë, she'd want me to open it no matter what. And since so few of her plans had turned out as she'd hoped, I wasn't about to disappoint her now.

I remove the bow gently, smiling as I tuck it behind my ear, remembering how Zoë and I always used to do that on Christmas morning, posing together like two Tahitian goddesses, red and green ribbons woven through our hair, while our dad stood before us, taking our picture. Then I slip my finger under the tape, taking more care than usual not to rip the paper as I unfold the edges, lift the lid, and retrieve the diary.

When I open it, the first thing I see is Zoë's familiar loopy scrawl:

Happy 14th b-day Echo!

And then right below that:

May your days be filled with excitement and fun, and may you record it all here!

Then I unwrap the candle, bringing it to my nose and inhaling its still surprisingly warm scent. Then I replace all the shoe boxes, putting them back the way they were, before going to my room, depositing her gift on my bed, removing all of my clothes, and heading for the shower.

And just as I'm closing the door, my cell phone rings. But knowing it's either Abby or Jenay, or maybe even Marc, I just turn the taps up even higher, letting the spray beat hard and hot against my back as I sink down to the ground, bring my knees to my chest, shield my face from the deluge, and finally let myself cry.

I never cry. Even at Zoë's funeral, when everyone was falling all over each other, falling all over themselves, I wore dark sunglasses, a stiff upper lip, and refused to give in to any of that. I guess I've never been comfortable with public displays of emotion. Because those kinds of moments, where I let myself cave and totally lose control, are always saved for when I'm alone. I mean, they're really no one's business.

And with my parents being such absolute basket cases, I knew even then that someone had to stay strong. And since it obviously wasn't going to be them, I figured it had to be me. Besides, the last thing I needed was for a bunch of relatives, people who hadn't seen Zoë since she was a baby, hugging all over me, crying on my shoulder, and giving their heartfelt condolences for a loss they could never begin to imagine.

And even though I know that may sound awful, the truth is that no matter how sorry everyone may have been, there wasn't a single person on the planet who could ever understand how I felt about Zoë. How much I missed her. And the huge gaping hole she'd left in my heart.

But now, with everything veering so out of control, I know I can no longer go it alone. But wouldn't you know it, Marc, the one person I trusted enough to turn to, turns out to be one person I never should've gone near.

When the water starts to run cool, I turn off the taps, dry off with a towel, then slip on a pair of my favorite old sweats. Then I pull my wet hair back into a tight ponytail and head down the stairs to the couch in the den, tucking the afghan tightly under my feet and picking up the diary from where I left off.

Twenty-nine

August 24

Everything started off great. Marc picked me up and he looked so good in his blazer and jeans, and I wore my cool new jeans, some strappy sandals, and my favorite cobalt blue halter top, then we drove to the restaurant where we sat at a nice table in the corner of this tiny but romantic plant-filled patio. And after ordering some appetizers and a couple of Cokes, I leaned toward Marc and smiled and said, "Is there something going on that I should know about?"

And he just looked at me all innocent and went, "What do you mean?"

And I knew I had a choice. I could either act all coy and beat around the bush until one of us gave in, or I could just get right to it and tell him how I know he's been holding out on me. So I said, "I know you're hiding something from me and I want to know what it is."

And instead of getting mad or curious, he just said, "Okay." Then he took a sip of his Coke and gazed around the room.

And no way was I about to leave it at that and allow him to blow it off so easily. So I said, "Marc, really, I'm totally serious. The last couple times when you told me you were home, I know for a fact that you weren't. And there's this one time in particular when I called and called but you never once answered even though you said you were there."

Okay, the second it was out I cringed at how needy and overbearing that sounded. I even wondered why I couldn't have waited 'til after our dinner, or even 'til tomorrow or something. But since it was already out there, I figured I may as well continue, so I looked at him and said, "Well?" Then I kicked the tip of my sandal against the table leg as I waited for his reply.

But it never came, he just shrugged.

So I went, "But what I'm really talking about is this one time in particular, when you told me you were home, but then I actually saw you," and then I paused because the waitress had just brought our appetizers. I didn't want her to hear any of this and know that we're kind of arguing since when she first came to our table I told her all about how it was our anniversary. But then the second she left I leaned in and said, "But I know you weren't home. And I happen to know that, because I saw you somewhere else."

But he just went, "Yeah?" And then he shrugged and grabbed a shrimp by the tail, dunked it in that red cocktail sauce, and then popped it into his mouth.

And I started to get so worked up by his acting so blasé and unconcerned about lying to me that I shook my head, leaned in even more, and loud whispered, "I saw you at the office where I work. And since my boss is on vacation, that means you were there to see Dr. Kenner."

But he just said, "I think you're confusing me with someone else." Then he grabbed another shrimp, popped it in his mouth, and smiled at me with the tail all caught between his teeth, like that was actually funny or something.

But when I refused to laugh, he started to look worried. And I knew I better just go for it and get it over with, since I was clearly teetering on the edge of either a total confession, or a full-blown fight. So I said, "Marc, listen, don't even try to lie or cover it up, cuz I know for a fact it was you."

He just stared, then he set down his fork and said, "And how exactly do you know that, Zoë?"

And that's when I told him about reading his file. And how I know all about his juvenile arrest and violent background and the fires and stuff.

I can hear my cell phone ringing from all the way upstairs, but no way am I going to stop reading just so I can answer it. But when the house phone also starts to ring, like the second the other one stops, I know it's my mom, which means I've no choice but to pick up.

"Hey Mom," I say, trying to make my voice sound all thick and groggy and sick, yet not so sick that she'll rush home to save me.

But it's Marc who says, "Echo, it's me."

And my heart starts pounding hard in my chest, partly because I can't imagine why he'd risk calling me on this line, and partly because I can't imagine why he's calling me in the first place. I mean, not after last night. But still, I'm determined to sound cool, calm, and relaxed so he'll never guess just how spooked he's making me feel, so I clear my throat and say, "Oh hey, what's up?" Seemingly all normal, like it's just another day.

"Well, it's lunch, and since you're not here with me, and

since you're not at your old table with your friends, I figured you might be home. You feeling okay?" he asks in a voice that actually sounds concerned.

"Why are you calling me on this line?" I ask, choosing not to answer his question about whether or not I'm okay, since I'm really not sure of the answer myself.

"Because you didn't answer your cell," he says, sounding pretty matter-of-fact.

"But what if my parents answered? What would you do then?"

"I don't know. Hang up?" He laughs. "I guess I just assumed they were still at work, which means you're home alone, right?"

I'm not sure why, but I don't want him to know the answer to that. So I take a deep breath and say, "Maybe."

Which just makes him laugh even more. "Fine. Listen," he says. "I'm sorry about last night. And I'm totally willing to blow off the rest of my classes so I can come over and see you. I think it's time I explain a few things, I think it's the least I can do."

"There's really nothing to explain," I say, wanting to sound blasé, but coming off more like edgy, paranoid, and totally freaked. Knowing I need answers, but not willing to get them from him.

"Trust me, there's plenty to explain. But I need to do it in person. I need you to understand. So is it okay if I come over?" he asks.

I grip the phone tightly, partly because my hand is totally shaking and partly because practically all of me is shaking. Then I take a deep breath and say, "No."

Then I hang up the phone, and check all three dead bolts.

Thirty

Since I'm already up, I go into my room and grab my cell, scrolling through the missed calls and finding one from Marc and one from Teresa, but nothing from Abby or Jenay, which makes me feel even worse than I thought it would. Then I put on some old, thick socks, 'cause I can't stand it when my feet get cold, and bring my phone back to the den, where Zoë's diary is waiting.

"What do you mean you read my file?" His jaw was all clenched and his eyes blazed with so much anger he was actually starting to scare me.

And with everything out there in the big wide open, I knew it was time to explain. "Listen," I said. "Promise you won't get mad and think that I'm checking up on you or spying on you or something, okay? But the truth is you've been acting really weird lately, lying to me, keeping secrets, and don't even try to deny it 'cause we both know it's true. And then when I saw you going into the office that day, the same day you said you were home, well, it made me really suspicious."

The second I gazed up at him I knew it wasn't going so well. So I started talking even faster, just hoping to get through it before something really bad happened. "And then Carly said we should go to the office and get to the bottom of it, though it's not like I'm blaming Carly or anything, I mean, obviously, the choice was all mine. So, well anyway, we went and let ourselves in, and when I saw Dr. Kenner was there we almost fled, but when he saw me he was all, 'Oh Zoë, excellent. My assistant just called out sick for tomorrow, so would you mind filling in? I know you're on vacation, but I'll pay you double to just answer the phone and let people in, and it's only for half the day since my wife can take over in the afternoon, blah blah blah, what do you say?' So I said yes. But then as it turned out I only had to stay for like forty-five minutes, 'cause his wife got there way early, though it was still long enough for me to read the first few pages of your file."

I stopped, looked up at him, and held my breath.

"So you read my file," he said, more like a fact than a question, and his lips were all pressed together and his eyes looked grim. "Or excuse me, only part of my file. Only the first few pages," he added, his voice sounding sarcastic and mad.

And it's not like I didn't already feel pretty horrible about doing that, but hearing him say it out loud made me feel even worse.

"I can't believe this shit," he said. "I can't believe you!" Then he threw his napkin down, pushed his seat away, and acted like he was about to storm out or something.

"What're you doing?" I whispered, glancing around frantically, just as the waitress appeared with our meals.

"I'm outta here," he said, as she just stood there, gaping at us, and holding our plates, probably thinking, And a BIG happy anniversary to you too!

"You can just take that away and bring me the check," Marc said, speaking to her, even though his eyes were fixed on mine.

I watched the waitress leave, then looked at him and said, "Fine. Just let me call my dad then. I'm sure he'll be willing to come pick me up, especially when I explain to him why." My face felt all hot as my eyes clogged with tears, and I was hoping that if nothing else, that would make him feel bad.

Well it must've worked cuz he just sighed and said, "Leave your parents out of this. You know I'll take you home." Then he shook his head and flipped through the bills in his wallet, throwing down more than enough to cover our appetizers, Cokes, and uneaten meals.

Then we left the restaurant and got into the car, neither one of us speaking the entire way home. And with each passing street, I felt sicker and sicker, knowing full well that I'd gone way too far, but still hoping for some kind of answer.

But when he got to my house he just hit the brakes.

And as I opened the door I looked at him and said, "I just don't understand why you feel like you can't trust me enough to confide in me."

But he just shook his head and said, "I think you just proved it."

August 29

Well, I guess the fact that we haven't talked for days means we either broke up or that we're on a break, which, no matter how you slice it, is basically the same damn thing. And while part of me is totally bummed by the fact that he ditched me, the other part, the smarter part, knows it's completely my fault.

But still, with my vacation ending, summer ending, and only one final week left at my job, I guess maybe it's pretty much the end of a lot of things, including us. Even though I really hope that's not true.

But for now I'm just gonna try to work as much as I can, save as much as I can, try not to dwell on the whole mess with Marc, and finally get around to contacting that photographer guy so I can get his rates and see just how much my big lifelong dream is gonna cost me. But the one good thing is that with Marc out of the picture, all of those things just became that much easier.

I just wish I didn't miss him so much.

Sept 9

Okay, so I haven't written in awhile because a lot has been happening, and I've been way too busy to write it all down. For starters, my job recently ended, with a hand-shake, a glowing report for my parents, a good reference for my resume (like anyone in Hollywood is going to care), and a nice, fat bonus check—yay me!

And then school started, which, surprisingly, isn't nearly as bad as it sounds, except for the fact that I keep running into Marc practically everywhere I go, and since he still won't talk to me, it can get kind of awkward.

Also, I e-mailed that photographer guy and he got right back to me, and the good news is he's way more affordable than I thought he would be. And just as I was about to schedule an appt for next week, Carly goes, "Um, maybe you want to hold off for a while, you know, so you can work out a little first."

Which made me go, "Excuse me, are you calling me fat?"

But she just shook her head and said, "No, of course not! But what I am saying is that skinny means different things in different cities. Like thin in New York and L.A. is probably way totally different than thin here. You know, like a Saks Fifth Avenue versus Wal-Mart kind of thing."

And the more I thought about it, the more I realized she was probably right. So I decided to give myself ten to twelve days of laying off the chips and Cokes and pot smoking (since pot smoking makes me crave chips and Cokes), and start actually participating in PE (as opposed to my usual avoidance of all things physical), and start swimming laps in Carly's pool (as opposed to lazing around and eating chips and drinking Coke and smoking pot).

I'm also trying to lose a little bit of my tan. Not all of it mind you, but definitely some of it. Because as Carly pointed out, the models in Vogue are always way skinny and way pasty, yet in Hollywood the celebs are all way skinny (not counting the implants) and way tan. And since I'm basically interested in doing either if not both, I figure it's probably better if I strive for somewhere in between.

Anyway, I'm really excited about this upcoming shoot, and have even been playing around with some possible outfits and hairstyles so I can show different looks and different sides to my personality and stuff. But then Carly said I should strive for pretty, unadorned, and natural, like Kate Moss in the early days. She says they mostly want chameleons who can easily change from season to season, and even though I have no idea how she actually knows all this stuff, since it's not like she cares about being a model or a movie star, I still gotta admit it makes perfect sense.

And even though I kind of wish I could share all this with Marc, I know it's probably all for the best. I mean, especially since it's not even an option anymore. Especially now that I keep seeing him hanging with that Shauna chick. And I don't mean hanging like they're all casual and stuff, because, please, it's not like I'm some psychotic jealous person. It's more the way that they're hanging, they way they act when they're talking. Like him leaning toward her, and her all happy and smiling and stuff. Like there's no one else around. Like they're in their own little world.

Just like we used to be.

The first time I saw them together I just stood there gaping, my mouth hanging open, my chin on my knees. And when she reached out and touched him, placing her hand right there on his shoulder, I was consumed with this indescribable, jealous, flood of rage. But eventually it mostly passed.

I mean, clearly we're not together anymore, no longer a couple. And it's time I get used to it.

Sept 10

Good news! Carly has finally stopped with all those crazy Web page hookups and trolling for alcohol with all those perverted geezers she was meeting on the Internet, and I could not be more relieved. Though it's not like she stopped because she figured out that what she was doing was dangerous, stupid, and completely freaking lame.

Nope, it was mainly because she met someone better. Someone who she thinks is hot, sexy, and a total keeper. Someone who rarely makes her pay, and when he does it's at a deeply discounted rate. He also happens to live in our town, even graduated from our high school. Though to be honest, I'm really not so sure that he actually graduated, because he doesn't seem like the type to heed authority or wear a cap and gown, so he might've just stopped going.

Anyway, his name is Jason—don't know his last— and I guess if you were standing really far away, with no binoculars, and were also very drunk, you might think that he's hot. Or at least that's what I thought the first time I met him. He's definitely kind of snakelike with that slicked-back hair, lean muscled body that he crams into these fitted faded jeans, black leather jacket, and motorcycle boots he always wears. But I guess he's kind of starting to grow on me too, since there's just something about him, something kind of alluring and dangerous and sleazy but cool. Which I know probably sounds pretty weird and all, but I don't know how else to explain it. Not to mention how he pretty much knows everyone in this town, or at least all of the people who party, and so far he's been more than willing to hook Carly up with whatever it is that she wants.

Anyway, the other night Carly and I ended up over there, just hanging out and talking with a whole group of people, and pretty much everyone was drinking but me (since I don't need the extra calories, not to mention the puffiness before the big shoot), and I was just kicking back and sipping from my water bottle, when he said, "Here, try some of these, they'll help you lose weight."

And I immediately looked at Carly, feeling all freaked and upset that she told him about my plans, because I really don't need a whole bunch of people to know about it before it's even had a chance to happen. But she just shrugged and shook her head, and motioned to me to go ahead and take 'em.

So then I looked at him, but he just laughed and said, "Pretty girl like you, avoiding the appetizers and beer and settling for just water, I figure you're just trying to stay pretty."

Okay, trying to pretend that smashed-up pieces of BBQ potato chips are actually appetizers is totally pushing it. But still, I took the bottle from him, and turned it around so I could squint at the back. Because let's face it, it's no secret that this guy is like our hometown version of Scarface, so the last thing I need is to get all hooked on crystal meth or something equally nasty that will make me skinny but leave me with no teeth.

But then he showed me where it says "All natural." And so with everyone watching and egging me on, I popped one in my mouth and chased it down with some water. And for the rest of the night everyone kept joking around and pretending that I was Alice through the Looking Glass, or Wonderland, or whatever (I mean, I really don't know the difference) and that I was getting smaller and smaller, 'til they could no longer see me.

And then, when it finally came time to leave, Jason kissed me on the cheek, his lips moving against my skin as he said, "You can thank me when you're posing on the cover of Maxim."

And even though Maxim isn't my number one goal (because that would be Vogue) it was still kind of cool to know that he thinks I have the potential. But I just smiled, and then the second I heard the door close behind us I rubbed my fingers over my cheek, removing the trace of his lips and wiping it onto my jeans.

Sept 14

So the last few days we've been hanging with Jason more and more after school, mostly because Carly is becoming a total burnout and is now totally hooked on some shit he sells her for cheap. And the only reason I even go along is so she doesn't go by herself, because she's seriously starting to worry me lately.

And then today, when I was walking home from school (by myself because Carly got detention for sneaking off campus and getting caught), he just happened to drive up and offer me a ride.

And I was just about to say no, 'cause I wasn't sure it was such a great idea to be in his truck alone with him, when I realized how totally stupid that was since I've been hanging with him like practically every day, and it's not like he's ever tried anything before. In fact, he's always been really super sweet. But even so, I was still about to say no, when I glanced over just in time to see Marc getting into his car and Shauna climbing in beside him.

So then I turned and looked at Jason, and said, "A ride would be great, thanks!"

And as I climbed up in his truck and closed the door, I glanced out the window just in time to see Marc staring at me. I mean serious, outright gaping. Just like I did when I first saw them. Then the light turned green, and Jason totally punched it, and in a matter of seconds they were left in our dust.

Sept 15

Jason picked me up from school again today, just like yesterday. Only this time he waited right there in the parking lot, instead of out by the corner like usual.

"Carly still on detention?" he asked.

And I just nodded and climbed in beside him.

At first he acted like he was going to drive me straight home, but then we somehow ended up at his apartment. Which even though it's not the first time I'd been there, it was the first time I'd been there on a bright sunny day, which just made it look even more shabby and messy than before. Not that I ever thought it was a palace or anything, but still, with the crappy stained couch and the dirty coffee table, it kinda makes you wonder where all the drug money goes.

So he grabbed a beer for himself and a glass of water for me, and even though he didn't actually make a move or try anything, I still felt kind of nervous to be sitting in the living room, just me and him, with no one else around. I mean, I found myself actually hoping for that retarded Tom guy to drop by, just to cut some of the tension.

I'm not sure why I was feeling like that, because obviously I'm free to do whatever with whoever. Though I think it's pretty obvious how hooking up with Jason would be a really bad idea. I mean, there are bad boys and then there are *bad* boys.

But since I didn't want him to know just how weirded out he was making me feel, I made a pact with myself that I'd be polite and hang for a half an hour or so, and then fake some excuse so I could bail out of there and make it home way before my parents.

He propped his boot-clad feet right on top of his filthy glass coffee table, then he started talking about a bunch of VIPs he claims to know in New York, L.A., and Vegas, and all kinds of other nonsense that really made me wonder if any of it could possibly be true.

And then for some reason I started to feel really really sleepy, and after like my third yawn in a row, he goes, "Am I boring you?"

And I felt so guilty I said, "No, of course not. I guess I just didn't sleep all that well last night, that's all." Which wasn't at all true, but still, I didn't want to be rude.

So then he said, "Well, why don't you lay down for a while and chill? I can take you home later." Then he smiled in a way that was trying to be more convincing than kind.

But I just shook my head and said, "No, I should probably get going. Do you mind taking me now?"

And right when he smiled and opened his mouth to speak, Carly knocked on the door.

"Hey, you guys. Got out early. Coach Warner got called away on some kind of family emergency, so he had no choice but to let us all go."

She plopped down on the couch, right beside Jason and smiled in a way that clearly showed how she didn't give a shit about the coach or his family. And it's not like I care about him either, I mean, so many times I've wanted to bust him for looking down my top, but still, a family emergency is never a good thing. Though in this case, I guess it was for Carly.

Jason immediately went to hand her his bong, but Carly just as quickly brushed it away. "Forget it. I've got to stop smoking. I'm getting fat, and my jeans are totally starting to strangle me," she said.

But he just laughed. "I got something to help you with that," he told her.

And she went, "What? They invented a Nicorette patch for burnouts?"

He smiled. "Even better."

"What, like those hippie herbal pills you give Zoë? No thanks," she said, shaking her head.

But he just got up and went into the kitchen (which is basically still in the same room, just over on the other side) and when he came back over he had these two pills in his hand. And when he gave them to Carly, she said, "What's this?"

And he smiled and said, "Zero-calorie, feel-good E."

And she goes, "Omigod, this is ecstasy? I've totally been wanting to try it." Then right before she places it on her tongue she squints at him and goes, "Wait, how much?"

But he just smiled and said, "Now baby you know me, the first three's always free."

So she grabbed my bottle of water and started to take them both, but before she could do that he grabbed her wrist and said, "Hold up, only one of those is yours. The other one's for Zoë."

And so she gave me the other one, and since I've always kind of wanted to try it too, and since I knew it would be safer if we did it together, I just popped it in my mouth then washed it down with a big swig of water.

It was only much later, on the way home, when I started to wonder if that was really E.

Sept 16

Okay, I didn't write this earlier because I'm really freaking out, and I'm not sure I even want to actually sit down and think about it, much less write about it. But at the same time I don't feel like I can allow this to just live in my head because it's starting to feel like way too much for me to hold on to. And since Marc's not around (not like I could ever tell him anyway) and since no way am I discussing it with Carly since she's partly responsible, I guess I'll just have to settle for here.

So let's just say that by the time Jason dropped me off, I was feeling like shit. I mean, seriously messed up and tired and clammy and nauseous, and just basically like total crap. And just as I was making my way up the drive, Marc stepped out from where he was waiting by the tree and said, "Did you have a good time?"

But I wasn't up for any of that. I was seriously upset, and all I wanted was to take a megahot long shower then go straight to bed. So I just shook my head and moved past him, intent on getting to the door without any more hassles, noticing how my mouth still tasted like vomit from when I got sick.

"I want to know if you had a good time with Jason," he said, grabbing my arm now, his fingers squeezing hard and tight.

And just as I was trying to yank my arm away, the

porch light went on and my dad opened the door, took one look at me, the way Marc was gripping my arm, and said, "Let go of my daughter."

So of course Marc immediately let go and started backing away. "I'm sorry," he said, both hands raised in surrender. "But you've got it all wrong. It's not what you think."

I just stood there, my forehead pressed against the door, my breath coming slow and weak, listening to my dad's voice, all hard and serious as he said, "I want you to get in your car and go home. And I don't ever want to see you anywhere near my daughter again, understood?"

And even though I wanted to explain how it wasn't at all like he thought, I couldn't. So I made my way upstairs and into my room, where I stripped off my clothes and went straight for the shower.

Great, my mom's knocking. Apparently it's dinnertime, so I guess I'll continue this later.

Later, though still Sept 16

So where was I? Oh yeah, so there are these bruises on my arm that my dad saw the next morning and just naturally assumed were from Marc. And even though I did my best to explain how he had it all wrong and how Marc would never ever do something like that, he still refused to believe me.

He just sat down beside me and gave me some lecture about Those Kinds of Guys. The kind who first charm you, then abuse you. He also told me that if he ever saw him near me again, then he'd . . . but thank G he just left that last part hanging.

And while in a way it was kind of sweet to see my dad get all protective and worked up like that—because let's face it, my family totally sucks at anything remotely *emotional—the fact is, it was all so misguided. Besides, it's not like I had any real faith in my dad's ass-kicking abilities. I mean, he'd seriously be lucky if he could bench-press an encyclopedia.*

Though it's not like I could even try to tell him the real truth. I mean, I'm barely willing to admit it to myself.

Because even though he thinks Marc's to blame, the truth is I know it's from what happened at Jason's. And the horrible things he made me and Carly do.

And even though I was so messed up that a lot of it's still pretty fuzzy, what I do remember really makes me wonder just exactly what it was that he gave us. Because only something really hard-core could get me to do what I did.

Especially in front of a camera.

I shut the diary and stare before me, unable to focus, my mind reeling from the things I'd just read—all the horrible things my sister endured, the secrets she kept that few people knew.

But I don't judge her. And not once while reading that did I shake my head and think, *You should've known better.*

Because Zoë's sweet, trusting nature was the biggest part of her. Her unruly optimism is what drew people to her. And it was unfortunate that not all of those people meant as well as she.

She warned me about Jason though, in her own indirect way. She called me into her room one day and showed me a photo she'd kept on her cell phone of her and Carly and some guy with slick blond hair and a black leather jacket. "You see this creep?" she'd said, stabbing his face with the tip of her fingernail. "Stay far away from him. I'm serious, Echo, promise me that if you ever see him somewhere you'll just turn around and walk the other way, okay? Promise?"

I leaned in and peered at the tiny thumbnail, then

shrugged and turned to leave. But she refused to let me off that easy, so she made me look again. Which is the only reason I recognized him in the park that first day.

Zoë was just trying to protect me, in the way that she failed to protect herself. She was always telling me to look out, to not be so trusting, to run away if my instincts suggested it, to act in a way that she didn't.

And it makes me wonder if maybe I'd been a year or so older, or even just acted a little more mature, if she would've eventually felt safe enough to confide in me.

But then again, probably not. Zoë always made it her job to protect me, even if it meant protecting me from herself.

I close my eyes, afraid of what else I might read, but knowing I need to continue. Then I think about Teresa and her infatuation with Jason, and grab my cell, knowing I have to try to warn her, even if she doesn't want to listen.

When she doesn't pick up, I leave a message. Then I chase it with a text, asking her to call me, explaining that it's urgent.

Thirty-one

Sept 17

For the last two days I've done my best to avoid Carly, which believe me, has not gone over so well. Especially after the bell rang and it was time to walk home and both times I didn't want to be anywhere near her. I mean, I'm sorry but I just can't go acting like everything's all fine and normal and like that whole disgusting day in Jason's filthy apartment never even happened. And the fact that she can just makes me want to avoid her even more.

So just when I thought it was safe, she saw me and was all, "Hey, wait up! Zoë, jeez! Are you avoiding me?" she asked as she ran to catch up with me.

I just took a deep breath and looked at her, having made up my mind not to lie. "Yes," I said, my eyes right on hers the whole time.

"And can I ask why?" She stood there, hands on hips, looking all mad and indignant and bitchy.

"Do I really need to explain?" I picked up the pace.

"Well, I guess not. But I really don't get why you're so freaked. I mean, what's the big deal? It's not like anyone will ever know."

I just looked at her and rolled my eyes, thinking she was so frustratingly lame, and wondering how we ever became friends. Then I said, "Well, you know what, Carly? I know. And you know. And Jason knows. And since he got it all on tape, it's just a matter of time before the whole freaking world knows! Don't you get it?"

But she just shrugged, like it's not a big deal, which made me even madder.

So I said, "I can't believe you did this to me. I can't believe you put me in that position!"

But she just goes, "It's not like anyone held a gun to your head, so stop acting like such a little effin baby. And let's just get one thing straight. Nobody made anyone do anything they weren't willing to do, okay? You were there of your own free will. Which means you also participated of your own free will."

But no way was I letting her off that easy, so I said, "Oh really, is it still free will if I'm all messed up on something he gave me? Something that I'm really starting to doubt was E? Because I think he gave us something else, Carly. I think he gave us something way worse."

But she just looked away and rolled her eyes, making it perfectly clear she thought I was overreacting. "Yeah? Well, it's not like he slipped it in your drink or anything. You took it right out of my hand, and nobody forced you to do that, Zoë."

And hearing her say that made me so mad I started to shake, probably because I knew in a way it was true. But also because I couldn't stop thinking about that glass of water he gave me, and how tired I felt after just a few sips. Though it's not like I could prove anything, and it's not like Carly would even care. So I just shook my head and said, "But still, don't you realize how messed up this all is? Don't you realize how this will all come back to haunt us? Stuff like this always does, there's just no avoiding it."

But she just rolled her eyes and went, "Relax, already. It's not like it hurt Paris Hilton's career. Or Pamela Anderson's. Or half of Hollywo—

But before she could finish that, I was already gone. And when I got to the parking lot, I saw Shauna kissing Marc.

And seeing them together like that made me burst into tears, and I took off running, just as fast as I could, wishing I could just keep going, just run without stopping 'til I reached the other side of the world.

Sept 19

My dreams are getting worse, and all the stress and lack of sleep is starting to make me look totally haggard. Seriously. I mean, my skin looks so bad I actually considered canceling the photo shoot. But then I realized how now more than ever I need to do whatever it takes to get the hell out of here so I never have to see Carly, or Jason, or anyone else in this stupid fucking town ever again.

I need to go somewhere new, someplace where I can start fresh. And then someday when I'm rich and famous, I'll get hold of that tape and destroy it.

Marc came up to me today at school, when I was standing at my locker, between classes. I was just switching out my books, when he leaned in and said, "Zoë."

That's it. All he said was my name, and I totally crumbled. Started bawling like a big pathetic baby. All of my worry, fear, and anxiety, all of my despair over the tape and my heartache over missing him and seeing how he'd already moved on to someone else, it all got mixed together and just came pouring out in a tsunami of emotion.

But he just held me close, keeping me tight against his chest as he stroked my hair and whispered in my ear. And when I still couldn't stop, he said, "Come on. Let's get out of here." Then he grabbed my hand and led me away.

We went to the park to feed our ducks. And at first we didn't speak much, but then once we got started, we could hardly stop. And I apologized for snooping in his file, and for getting so upset, and he apologized for getting so mad and avoiding me like that. Then just as I was feeling really really close to him, close enough to confide about the whole mess with Jason, he mentioned Shauna. Telling me how it didn't mean anything, how she was a nice girl and all, but still, a very poor substitute for me.

So I held my tongue, and didn't say a word. Reminding myself how he wouldn't really want to know, and how it was far better to just keep quiet.

Though I did say that if he wanted to be back together with me, then he was never allowed to call Shauna again. And he agreed.

Then he told me all about Dr. Kenner, and how he started seeing him way back when his dad first went to jail and his mom started boozing and sleeping around on a regular basis, and how he was so full of rage and anger that he basically went kind of nuts and ended up vandalizing one of the buildings at his private school. At first his mom was able to keep it quiet by paying for the damage, pulling him out, and enrolling him somewhere else, but at the next school it was basically the exact same thing, and it pretty much went on like that until they ran out of expensive schools. So I guess Bella Vista and Dr. Kenner were pretty much his last great hope, since if he messed up again he'd be headed straight to juvie, no matter how much money his mom threw at the courts.

He said it all worked out for the best though, since Dr. Kenner really helped him find his way through all the really bad stuff, and he learned how to control his anger and channel it into other things, like fixing cars and music and books and stuff like that. It's also part of the reason why he doesn't like to drink. He said now that he knows what it's like to be in control, he doesn't ever want to risk losing that again.

So I went, "But why didn't you tell me all this before? Why'd you keep it a secret?"

And he said, "I was about to tell you when I found out where you worked, but the way you made fun of the patients, well, I didn't want you to see me like that."

I just nodded, feeling so incredibly awful for being so insensitive and making him feel bad. And I also felt so guilty when I realized how he'd confided all of his secrets, but I was still keeping mine.

But then he said, "The only thing that could ever make me fly off the handle again is to see you anywhere near Jason. That guy is total trash, and I want you to stay away from him, okay?"

Then he held my chin, and made me face him. And his eyes were so dark and severe, I just nodded, and quickly looked away.

Later, when Marc drove me home, all the cars were gone so I invited him inside, and I found a note from my mom telling how she and my dad and Echo went for pizza and a movie and how they'd all be back later.

So it didn't take long for Marc to coax me upstairs, obviously looking forward to a little make-up sex. And even though at first I thought I wanted it too, once he started kissing me, I just couldn't go through with it.

But when I tried to roll over and push him away, wanting for him to just hold me and love me and keep me safe, he got upset.

"C'mon Zoë, I've missed you so much," he whispered.

But I ignored him and just closed my eyes, trying not to think about Carly and me and Jason's camera. Not to mention Shauna and Marc and what they might've done together.

"What gives?" he asked, kissing the back of my neck and reaching around for my breasts.

But I just pulled the covers over me, and said, "Nothing, jeez." Then I rolled my eyes, but it's not like he could see.

"Then why are you covering yourself?" he asked, refusing to just hold me and let the rest go.

"'Cause I'm cold," I said, going right back to lying again.

But it was clear he didn't believe me. "Does this have anything to do with Jason?" he asked. "Is there something I need to know?"

And even though every part of me was screaming YES, desperate to finally unload this burden so I wouldn't have to carry it alone, I knew that I couldn't. Because when I finally turned to face him, feeling ready and willing to talk, I saw that his eyes were dark and angry for the second time today.

And suddenly I understood how someone as sweet and mellow as he could set fires, break windows, and tear things apart. And all I wanted was for him to leave.

I turned so we were no longer facing each other, then I closed my eyes and said, "What's the matter, Marc, Shauna left you hanging too?"

Then he grabbed hold of my arms, but released them just as quickly. Then he got up from the bed, grabbed his clothes, and fled.

*And I lay there like that, 'til long after he left, wonder-
ing who I should fear more, Jason or Marc?*

I'm almost at the end. The end of the diary, the end of Zoë.
And even though I'm desperate to finish, I'm just as reluctant
to say good-bye. I gaze over at the clock, seeing how it's well
past two, and wonder if Abby and Jenay will talk about me on
the way home, or if they're so glad to be rid of me they've already moved on.

I still have time to burn before my mom comes home, and
you can pretty much double that for my dad. And wanting to
just take my time with the last few pages, I set it on the coffee
table and go outside.

Winter has already edged out fall, having moved in
quickly with its crisp cold air and warm clean scent of wood
fireplace logs—two things I always look forward to. And as I
walk around my mom's formerly well-tended but now much-
neglected garden, I notice how the spring blooms, having
gone completely ignored, are now either all shriveled up and
hanging by a sliver or rotting away on the ground, their stalks
bent down by their sides. And I wonder if my mom will ever
put on her hat and gloves and venture back out here, redis-
covering the things that once brought her such joy. Or if this
is how we'll always live now, just barely cared for but mostly
untended.

I shiver against the wind, my worn sweatpants, thin T-shirt,
and thick socks with the big gaping hole in the heel providing
a pretty pathetic shield. But still, it's not like I move for cover,
or even think about going inside. Instead I just stand there,
rubbing my arms for warmth, feeling grateful to have a problem with such an obvious solution.

Reading Zoë's diary has left me on shaky emotional
ground, and I feel like I'm living on a fault line, where my

moods rise and fall with every slight shift, while the world I'd once known quakes precariously around me.

So compared to all that, Old Lady Winter is pretty much a wimp.

I stay out a while longer, watching my neighbor's black cat delicately pick his way across the top of our fence before jumping down to the other side. Then I head for the door, closing it quickly behind me when I hear my phone beeping in the den, and someone banging hard against the front door.

Thirty-two

You'd think that at some point during my parents' marathon of paranoia, somewhere around the time when they were installing the third dead bolt, they would've noticed how the front door is surrounded by glass. And not stained glass, or bathroom glass, or any other kind of glass that has bumps and colors that do a fine job of distorting an image. Nope, I'm talking plain, old, clear glass, the kind you can see right through.

But somehow they missed that.

Which leaves me face-to-face with Marc.

"Hey," he says, waving from the other side. "It took you forever to answer and I was worried. Let me in."

I watch him standing there waving, part of me about to obey, while the other part freezes. And suddenly I wish I'd skipped the little backyard field trip and just finished that diary once and for all.

"Whose car is that?" I ask, gazing at a bright red, vintage MG now parked on my driveway.

"Let me in and I'll tell you," he says, nodding and smiling, so sure that I will.

But I just shake my head and turn away, moving back toward the den where I sit on the couch, listening as he bangs on the door, saying things like, "Echo, please. I can explain. I want to explain. But you have to let me in."

But I just pick up my cell to check my voice mail, breathing a sigh of relief when I hear Marc finally drive away.

"Echo, hey, it's so weird you called me and said that it's urgent and all, because I really need to talk to you too. So if you could, oh shit, here comes Ms. Jenkins." Then I listen as Teresa says in her sweet, obedient voice, "It's off! I swear, look!" And then she whispers, "Jeez, okay, anyway, it's about—hey, give it ba—!"

And even though her phone is most likely in Ms. Jenkins's possession, I dial her number anyway. But when she doesn't answer, I know the next move is hers.

Sept 21

I don't know what I was thinking when I scheduled this appointment, because if I thought I could just stroll off campus with a duffel bag full of makeup and clothes that I'd managed to hide all day from Marc by keeping it stashed in my gym locker, then shame on me because that was one stupid, not-so-well-thought-out plan.

And since I'm no longer talking to Carly, which means I'm not talking to Paula all that much either (since they're always together now), it's not like I had anyone left to help me pull this off. So I just figured that the second the final bell rang, I'd try to grab all my stuff and skip out.

But guess who was already there, standing by my locker, waiting?

Okay, I know I didn't write yesterday, cuz I was just way too busy getting everything organized, so let me just say that a couple hours after Marc left, he called to apologize, and then way later he came back over and I snuck him into my room and he just held me while I slept. And when I woke up in the middle of the night he was already gone, and then yesterday at school we both acted like none of the bad stuff ever happened, that I never said that shit about Shauna, and that he never got angry about Jason, and that we were never really broken up to begin with. And since that's the way I actually wanted things to be, it was pretty easy to play along and pretend.

And then late last night I snuck out and went to his place since his mom and stepdad are out of town, and we went skinny-dipping, hung in the Jacuzzi, then slept together in the bed in the pool house. Then just before the sun came up, he drove me home. And right before climbing back up the tree, I kissed him good-bye. And at that moment I knew I was being given a second chance, that we really could start over. I just hoped I would be smart enough not to blow it.

So anyway, this is the first time I've ever carried my diary with me, the first time I ever took it out of the house, and even though I keep kind of freaking out and double-checking to make sure I didn't lose it (I mean, can you even imagine?), today is such a humongo big day that I just feel like I should document every single second of it, since it's the first day of taking the first step toward changing my entire life! Not to mention how when I become really rich and famous, they'll probably ask me to write my memoirs, and I can use this as a guide.

Anyway, I feel so incredibly good about this meeting—I've lost six pounds, not that I even needed to, but since the camera does add ten, I figure it can't hurt—and I even found this amazing new cover stick that is totally working at hiding the dark circles and all the other signs of worry, stress, and major lack of sleep. And it's just so amazing how it's all falling so smoothly into place. I mean, before all this came together, I was never all that big on destiny. I mean, yeah, I would joke about it and stuff, but that doesn't mean I actually really believed in it. I just always figured that you get to where you want to go by working hard and totally going for it—not by any kind of cosmic energy, or whatever. But now, with the way it's all moving forward, I just know deep down inside that it's totally meant to be.

So anyway, when Marc saw me at my locker with my overstuffed bag, he just looked at me, and said, "What's that?"

Well, at first I tried to lie and tell him I was getting a bunch of clothes taken in since I'd lost all that weight. But when it was clear he wasn't buying it, I told him I was auditioning for a play, and that I was too freaked out, nervous, and superstitious to say anything more about it.

"Just a community theater thing, no biggie. I'm just doing it for the experience," I said.

"Can I come?" he asked.

But I told him no. Told him that he'd make me too nervous, and that I didn't even want him to drive me. I'd just planned to take the bus, which meant I needed to leave right away, since it'd take me a whole lot longer to get there like that (which isn't even a full lie, because I had planned to take the bus to the photo shoot).

So he just looked at me and said, "How 'bout I drive you and pick you up after?"

And I said, "No way, Jose. In fact, I don't even want to talk about it afterward, unless of course they cast me, then I'll bore you to death with all the details."

So he goes, "Well then how 'bout this—we go to the

park, hang for a while, and then you take my car and come pick me up when you're done?"

"But I don't know how long it will take! I mean, you're just gonna sit there that whole time?" I asked, part of me really wanting the car since it would make everything so much easier, but the other part not wanting to be responsible for picking him up. I mean, what if it runs late? But still, having the car will really help, so I agreed.

Okay, so I just wrote all that in the parking lot of the Circle K, where he just went in to get us some snacks and waters and cigarettes and bread for our pet ducks. And now he's back so—

"Thank you darling," I say, wanting a ciggie big-time but knowing I can't write and open the pack at the same time. But really, what's more important, smoking or recording all the little mundane things that happen to me while I'm still anonymous?

So he goes, "What are you writing about that's making you so happy?"

Then he acts like he's trying to peek over my shoulder, so I pull it away and say, "You have no idea."

So we're at the park now, and I'm feeding the ducks while Marc starts on his homework and then he looks at me and goes, "So what play are you trying out for?"

And since I'm more into movies, and don't really know any plays, I go, "Phantom of the Opera." And believe me, the second it's out, I regret it.

So he looks at me and goes, "I didn't know you could sing opera." Then he gives me this suspicious squinty kind of look.

But I think I pulled it off, cuz I just said, "I don't, silly. It's for a nonsinging part. A really small part, in fact, and it's really no big deal. I just think it will be good experience to go to an audition and see what it's like to be onstage with everyone watching you and stuff." And since it seems like he might actually believe that I add, "But what about you? Are you really just gonna sit here and wait?"

And he smiles and goes, "Yup."

And I go, "But what if you get bored, or need to go home or something?"

But he just shakes his head and says, "No worries, I'll handle it. Just don't forget to come back for me." Then he jangles his car keys as he starts to hand them over.

And I go, "Please, I could never forget you," then I lean in and kiss him, and reach for the keys.

But then he goes, "Wait, I want something in return."

I just looked at him, thinking I should've known better, 'cause there's always a catch. "What?" I ask.

"Your diary," he says. "Leave me your diary just to make sure."

"Make sure of what?"

"To make sure you come back to me. You know, like collateral?" He smiles.

"You're not gonna read it, are you?" I ask, still wanting those keys but not liking the trade, and wondering if I can trust him to really not read it.

But he just gives me a serious look, and says, "Only if you don't come back." Then he leans in and kisses me, and says, "And when you return, I have a major surprise for you. Something you're gonna love, that will also explain everything, everything you've been wondering about where I was those times when you couldn't reach me. I just want us to rewind, to get back to where we were. I really love you, Zoë."

So I say, "And I really love you, Marc."

Then he smiles and says, "Are you ever going to stop writing so I can kiss you and tell you good-bye?"

And I smile and say, "Yes!"

I turn the page but that's it. And every page that follows is as blank as the one before it, nothing but blue lines on white background, Zoë's loopy handwriting coming to its final rest.

I close my eyes and lean back against the cushions, tears pouring down my cheeks, thinking how strange it is that her diary ended on "Yes!" When her life probably ended on "No!"

I sit there, holding her book in my lap, unwilling to look at it, unable to let go.

And when my cell phone rings, I hit *speaker,* wiping my eyes as Teresa says, "Echo, I'm on my way over. We really need to talk."

Thirty-three

Seconds later when the doorbell rings, I assume Teresa was a lot closer than I'd thought. But when I peek through the glass and see Abby, my stomach drops so fast and hard it takes me a moment to realize that she's smiling as though yesterday never happened.

"Jeez, you really are sick. You look awful," she says, giving me a concerned once-over while maintaining a safe distance from any potential infectious disease.

"Relax, I'm fine," I tell her. "Seriously, it's safe to come in."

She gives me a hesitant look then steps inside, following me into the den, where she flops down on my dad's favorite chair, and goes, "So, what gives?"

But I just shake my head and sit on the couch, pulling the afghan around me, hugging my knees tight to my chest. "I've been going through some stuff," I finally say, knowing I owe her much more than that, but feeling unsure just how far I should go.

"I know." She nods.

"You know?" I ask, looking at her and wondering just how much she knows.

"Well, for starters, you've been acting pretty freaky since the first day of school. And then all that stuff yesterday, well, that was pretty much the pinnacle of your freakiness."

"Does Jenay hate me?" I ask.

She laughs. "Jenay's incapable of hate. She's all about love, pep rallies, and cheerleading tryouts."

"Seriously?"

"'Fraid so." Abby nods. "Tryouts are months away, but she's already talking about it. She wants to be able to cheer for Chess at all of his football games."

"Can't she do that from the stands?"

"Not like a professional." She smiles.

"So, do *you* hate me?" I ask, holding my breath.

"Honestly? I did. But then I got over it." She shrugs. "Because I know what you're going through. Okay, backtrack. Maybe I don't know *exactly* what you're going through. But sometimes I try to imagine it, you know? Like when Aaron's driving me nuts and I'm fantasizing about totally throttling him. Well, sometimes I make myself stop and imagine how I'd feel if he was no longer around for me to hate. And the truth is, as much as he annoys me, I know it would be a whole lot worse without him. And then that makes me think how bad it must suck for you to have to deal with all that, not to mention the way people stare and the things they say. And I don't mean like I pity you," she says quickly, knowing full well just how much I hate to be pitied. "It's just, I don't know, I guess I just want you to know that I care, and that I'm here, and that no matter how hard you try, you can't push me away. Or maybe

you can, but you're gonna have to try a lot harder than that."
She smiles, but her bottom lip is trembling. And seeing that
makes me feel unbelievably sad, especially when I realize how
willing I was to discard her.

"So where is Jenay?" I ask, anxious to change the subject.

"Pep club," she says, rolling her eyes. "But one more thing,
Echo, and then I promise to let it go. I just want you to know
that you can totally confide in me if you need to. Seriously, you
can tell me anything you want and I promise not to judge or
ever repeat a single word of it to anyone, including Jenay.
Scout's honor." She holds up her hand, palm facing forward,
even though we were never Scouts.

And when I look at her, I'm tempted, thinking how nice it
would be to get some of this burden off my chest, not to have
to bear all this weight on my own. But when I start to speak, I
realize there's still a few missing links, and I know I should
wait 'til I've gathered all the pieces.

So instead, I just shrug. "Rain check?" I ask, smiling as she
nods.

When the doorbell rings a few minutes later, this time it really
is Teresa. And when she comes in the den and sees Abby still
sitting in the chair she gives me a quick, worried look.

"I should probably go," Abby says, rising from her seat in
a rare display of submission.

I glance at Terersa, wondering if she'll insist on it, but she
just shrugs and sits on the floor.

"Oh my God." She drops her head in her hands and rubs
her eyes with the pads of her fingers. "I've been so fucking stupid and I owe you the hugest apology," she says, finally looking up at me, her eyes red and worried.

I glance at Abby, who's clearly wondering what this is

about, then I gaze back at Teresa when she says, "I need to talk to you about Jason."

"Who's Jason?" Abby asks, but when I look at her and shake my head, she goes quiet and leans back in her chair.

"Jason is a creep," Teresa says, gazing at Abby and shaking her head. "A total freaking psychotic creep. Echo tried to warn me, but I was too stupid to listen. I thought he was some sexy, exciting, bad boy. Turns out he's just bad."

"Are you okay? I mean, did he hurt you?" I ask, remembering what happened to Zoë and Carly, and hoping that didn't happen to her.

But she just shakes her head and closes her eyes, and when I glance over at Abby I can tell she's confused. "Well, you know how normally we just meet up at the park and hang out and stuff? Like we did that one day? And how every now and then he'd stop by my house and we'd party when my parents weren't home? Well, we did fool around, but only a few times, nothing major, basically because asshole Tom was usually there."

I glance at Abby when she starts to say, "Who's asshole To—" But then she looks at me and shakes her head, motioning for Teresa to continue.

"So yesterday, I was on my way home from school when he drove up and offered me a ride. And since no one was around to see me, I opened the door and got in."

"Did you go to his place?" I ask, remembering Zoë and how he used the same M.O. on her.

She rolls her eyes and nods. "Jeez, you should see it, I mean, it's a total freaking dump. I mean a filthy, cheap, disgusting mess."

And just as I start to say, "I know," I remember how I do know, and not wanting to share that with them, I don't say anything.

"So he offers me a beer, and like the idiot I am, I'm all excited that we're finally gonna hook up, since we're all alone and stuff. So, thinking I should go freshen up a little first, I head for his bathroom as he heads for the fridge, and then I notice how the bathroom door is like right across from his bedroom, and I'm really tempted to open the door and take a look, but I'm also afraid of getting caught. So instead I just go inside and do my thing and right as I come out, I see him sitting on the couch with his index finger all shoved down the neck of my beer bottle. And I think, *what the heck is he doing?* And I start to feel all creeped out, wondering if he's trying to poison me or drug me or something. So then I get all panicked, wondering what I should do. But then I decide to just act all smiley and calm until I can eventually find a way out of there." Then she stops and looks at Abby and goes, "Do you think you can get me some water?"

And before I can even say anything, Abby is already up and heading for the kitchen. Teresa turns to me and whispers, "So anyway, I just try to act all normal, tapping my bottle against his, taking fake sips, and then right when I'm about to make an excuse to get out of there, his beeper goes off. So he goes, 'I have to run out for a sec, so sit tight and don't go snooping around.' And when he gives me this threatening look, I just smile and nod and take another fake sip, and then like the second he leaves I'm about to bail, but then I wonder if maybe I'm overreacting. I mean, maybe he was just fishing a bug out of my beer, which is still pretty bad, though it's not the same as drugging someone, right?"

Abby comes back with the water, and after taking a quick sip, Teresa looks at me and hesitates. "Should I continue?"

And since I have no idea where this is going, I really don't know how to answer. But I also don't feel like I can just kick Abby out, not after the way I've treated her. So I just shrug, letting Teresa decide. Then she takes another sip and goes,

"Okay, so anyway, I decided to check out his bedroom, since the fact that he warned me not to snoop just made me want to do it even more. But then the second I open the bedroom door, I know where all of his money goes." She looks at us and rolls her eyes. "He's got this huge, four-poster bed, with these serious-looking, black leather restraints attached to all the posts, and there're these two video cameras on tripods, and they're both pointing right at the bed. I mean, there's got to be like thousands of dollars' worth of video equipment in there, like he's making home porn or something. Anyway, I got so freaked out, and I knew I had to get out of there while I still could, and just as I was about to leave I noticed this huge stack of videos all lined up on a shelf, each one labeled with different girls' names." She looks at Abby, then me, and takes a deep breath. "And when I saw the one labeled 'Zoë/Carly,' well, I just grabbed it and ran."

She shakes her head and looks at me. "I didn't sleep the entire night cuz I was so scared about everything that happened, and everything that could've happened, and what he might try to do to me if he notices the missing video. And I really needed to see you, but then when you didn't come to school today . . ." She shrugs, looking back and forth between me and Abby.

I glance at Abby, who's sitting there completely still, her eyes wide, her mouth hanging open, then I look at Teresa and say, "What'd you do with the tape?" And I watch as she reaches into her big green tote bag, then hands it to me.

"You should burn it," she says. "You should get rid of it so no one will ever find it."

I turn it over in my hands, wondering if I will.

"I'm so freaking scared," she says, starting to cry now. "I mean, what if he notices it's missing, then tries to come after me and retaliate or something?"

I close my fingers around the tape, pressing it hard into

my palm. Then I look at her and say, "You have to call the cops. You have to make sure he pays."

"I know," she whispers, nodding her head, her eyes filled with tears.

"But then everyone's gonna know your business, and everyone's gonna talk."

But she just shrugs. "I know that too."

Thirty-four

The second Abby and Teresa leave, I run up to my room and shove the diary and tape between my mattress and box spring, placing them side by side, having no idea what to do with them but wanting them out of my sight. Then I pace back and forth between my bed and the french doors, wondering what I should do.

On the one hand, I know they contain evidence of yet another horrible crime against Zoë. Something she felt not only responsible for, but terribly ashamed of. And it makes me so sad to know that she viewed it that way, because even though he didn't hold a gun to her head, Jason still drugged her and tricked her into doing something she never would've otherwise done. Not to mention that he's an adult, one who was well aware of the fact that Zoë and Carly weren't.

But I also think my sister had been through enough. And

I'm not sure I can drag her memory—not to mention my parents—through all of this too.

"I'm gonna go to the cops and tell them everything," Teresa had said as she stood on my porch, right before leaving. "But I won't say a word about Zoë. I swear. I mean, there's probably plenty of evidence to convict him, so I doubt they'll even need it. Besides, I feel like I owe you, I mean you did try to warn me and all."

"What do you think I should do?" I asked, looking from her to Abby, who for practically the first time ever had no advice to give.

"Forget it," she'd said, raising her hands in surrender. "I'm out. This stuff is way over my head. I had no idea you guys were living these dangerous, top-secret lives."

I looked at Teresa, but she just shrugged. "Up to you. But I promise not to say anything you don't want me to."

And as I closed the door behind them, I remembered Marc, and I knew I had to find him.

I flip open my cell and dial his number, listening to it ring so many times, I'm about to give up. But when he finally does answer, I get straight to the point. "I'm sorry," I say. "For so many things. But I really need to see you now, and it's actually pretty urgent. Do you think you can come by?"

He tells me he will, without once asking why.

I throw my peacoat over my ratty old sweats, shove my feet into some boots, pull a beanie onto my head, wrap a long, wool scarf twice around my neck, then reach under the mattress and grab the video, slipping it deep into my coat pocket. Then I purposely avoid looking in the mirror as I unlock my french doors and reach for the tree.

Obviously, I'm not trying to look cute for Marc. Because whatever weird attraction passed between us is now clearly over. At least it is for me. And I'm pretty willing to bet that it is for him too.

Because I think I finally get how my trying to be like Zoë—and Marc and I trying to be together—was just one more failed attempt to save her. And the truth is, Zoë is dead. And even though it's almost unbearable to finally admit to the "D" word, if I truly want to move on then I can no longer avoid it.

But now I'm wondering if there might be another way to save her. Now I'm wondering if I should just burn this tape and save her from yet another starring role as the poster child for bad choices. Or if maybe I should turn it in, so they can add it to the stack of evidence and make sure Jason pays.

But the weirdest thing is, I feel like it's Marc who can finally help me. Out of all the people I know, he's the only one who can help me decide.

I reach for the thickest branch, grabbing hold of it with both hands even though it would be a whole lot easier just to go downstairs and use the front door. But I know this is probably the last time I'll ever do this. And because of that, I want to get it just right.

I swing my body toward the trunk, gripping it between my knees and hugging it firmly as I shimmy all the way down to the ground, so quickly and effortlessly it's as though Zoë's right there beside me, nodding encouragingly and cheering me on.

Then I run to the corner and wait, blowing on my hands since I forgot to wear my gloves, and jumping from foot to foot in an attempt to stay warm. And when a bright red MG pulls up and brakes right beside me, it's a moment before I remember it's Marc's.

"Hey," he says, leaning over and opening the door. "You okay?"

I nod my head and climb inside, grateful for the warmth of the car and the strange comfort he provides. "I'm sorry about earlier, I just—"

But he just shakes his head and lifts his hand to stop me. "No worries," he says, pulling away from the curb and turning onto the next street.

But I don't want to be cut off like that. I mean, I owe him an apology. Lots of people owe him an apology. But I can only speak for me. "I finished her diary," I tell him, forcing myself to look right at him, even though it makes me feel a little uncomfortable. "I guess I got a little caught up along the way, and I'm sorry about that. I'm sorry I doubted you, and I'm sorry my sister doubted you, and I'm sorry this whole stupid town doubts you. But right now I need your advice, and you're the only one I can trust."

He parks in a spot that faces the lake, and we remain in the car, gazing quietly at the water before us until I take a deep breath and remove the tape from my pocket, presenting it in the palm of my outstretched hand.

"Where'd you get that?" he asks, his eyes turning dark, just like the other day.

"From Teresa," I say, my voice steady and sure, despite the erratic beating of my heart. "She swiped it from Jason's."

He grabs it, surrounding it with his fist and lifting his arm as though he's gonna toss it out the window or something. But just as quickly his body crumbles, his back hunched over in despair and defeat. "I should've known," he finally says, his head against his hands, his knuckles pressed to his forehead. "I should've fucking known."

"Known what?" I ask, my voice almost a whisper.

"That he kept a copy." He raises his head and stares at the lake. "I have now truly failed her in every single way."

"Don't," I say, reaching toward him, my hands fumbling, unsure, watching as he drops the tape onto his lap, his hands rubbing his eyes so roughly it scares me. "Don't say things like that. No one could have saved her, and it's time we all realized that. You read the diary, you know what I'm talking about."

But he just turns to me, his face red and raw, his eyes filled with pain. "That day at Teresa's?" he says. "When you were wondering what Jason gave me? What I had in my pocket? It was this. It was another copy of *this.*" He picks up the tape and shakes his head. "I *knew* something happened that day, but Zoë refused to tell me. Then about six months after her funeral, when the guy's finally caught and the whole media circus is getting a second wind, he calls me up to tell me that he's got something I might want, and how he's willing to sell it for just the right price. Only the price kept changing. And every time we'd meet he kept dicking me around for more and more money. Just naturally assuming that my parents' wealth had anything to do with me. I had to sell off all the bonds my grandparents gave me, using up all the money I was saving for Zoë's memorial. But that day at Teresa's, he finally settled. And I just kept telling myself the whole entire time that even though it may not be the memorial I'd planned, I was still pre-serving her memory." He laughs then, but it's not a funny laugh. It's more the cynical kind. The world-just-keeps-getting-worse-and-worse kind.

"Why didn't you just go to the police? They could've han-dled it for you," I say.

"Maybe I should've." He sighs. "But at the time, I just couldn't risk it. I mean, for Zoë, not me. You hear what people say, and I couldn't stand to put her through that again. Believe me, my life isn't all that important anymore. I only wanted to protect her."

"Don't say that," I urge, gripping his arm, but he won't look at me, he's back to facing the window again. "Zoë would've hated to hear you talk like that," I add. "You know it wasn't her fault, you know she never consented."

"Doesn't matter." He shrugs. "People believe what they want, and I just couldn't put her through that again." He turns to me, his eyes clouded with anguish.

"How much did you give him?"

He closes his eyes and shakes his head. "You don't want to know. Let's just say it was enough to wipe me out until I turn twenty-one and take control of my trust."

"What kind of memorial were you planning?"

He looks at me and smiles. And it's so nice to see his face like that I wish it could last. "A little bench. Placed right over there," he says, pointing toward the lake. "Right in front of the water, where we always used to sit. So that people can come and relax and feed all of her ducks for her."

I reach toward him then, cupping my hands around his cheeks, bringing his face toward mine. Then I close my eyes and kiss him. But not the same kind of kiss as before, not like I'm trying to claim something that was never meant to be mine. I kiss him lightly and quickly and briefly, because he loved my sister. And because he's paid such a high price for it.

When he drops me back at my house, he looks at me and says, "So what should we do with the tapes?"

I take a deep breath. "You know, there could be other copies," I say. Then I tell him about Jason and Teresa.

"Oh, God." He shakes his head and looks away.

"But I still think I should hand it over." And when I say that, I realize how I suddenly feel sure of myself for the very first time since I got involved in any of this. "Because what happened to Zoë isn't her fault. The only thing she's guilty of is having a dream. And I think we owe it to her to believe that."

He nods, then hands me the tape, and as I open the door and crawl out of the car, I say, "But last night, when you said that about 'hurting me too'? What did you mean?"

He looks at me, his eyes wet with tears. "I failed her, plain and simple. And by allowing myself to get involved with you, I failed you too." He gazes down at his hands, balling them into tight fists before letting them release and relax. "I still love her, Echo. And I miss her so much. I'm sorry I let things progress like I did. I should've known better." He wipes his eyes with the back of his hand and stares off into the distance.

"Thanks for sharing her," I say, smiling as he turns toward me, his eyes full of questions. "You were right, I didn't really know her. But now I do."

He presses his lips together and nods, and as I shut the door and turn away, I remember how there's still one last thing. So I knock on the window, and as he rolls it down, I say, "Hey, what was the surprise? You know, the thing you were holding for Zoë? For when she came back?"

He looks at me and smiles. "You're leaning on it," he says. Then seeing my confusion he goes, "All those days when I was unavailable and not answering her calls? I was actually holed up in my garage, working on this car. I bought it off my uncle, cheap, just so I could fix it up for Zoë. I thought a girl like her deserved something special, something nobody else had."

"It's beautiful," I say, standing back to admire it, taking in the spoke wheels, the wood dash, the cherry red paint job, and black, convertible cloth top. "She would've loved it." I smile.

But he just shrugs.

"So what are you gonna do with it?"

He shakes his head. "It mostly just sits in my garage, I barely ever drive it. Yet I've been unable to part with it, though I guess it's finally time. You want it?"

I gaze at the car, part of me wanting to claim it, knowing I may never own a car as amazing as this. But the other part knows it can be put to much better use. "Why don't you sell it and buy her that bench?" I say.

And when he looks at me he smiles. And he's still smiling as he drives away.

Thirty-five

Echo's Diary
<u>Do not disturb!</u>

Jan 10

Today the bench was finally unveiled, so we held a big party for Zoë. And even though some people still insisted on calling it a memorial, I refused to see it that way. We did that already, over a year and a half ago. So this was more like a celebration of her life, not another remembrance of her death.

At first my parents acted all weird around Marc, but probably just out of habit. Because now they finally get that no matter how much he loved her, he just couldn't save her. None of us could. And trying to blame anyone other than her killer is just a total waste of time.

So after a few awkward moments, my dad grasped

Marc's hand, his jaw going all tight and determined as he struggled not to cry. And my mom, off the happy pills for almost three months now and no longer scared or enslaved by her tears, hugged him tight to her chest while she smoothed his hair and whispered into his ear that it will all be all right.

Then my mom wiped her face and my dad nodded his head, and they reached for each other, holding hands and leaning together, finally finding strength in the one place it'd been waiting all this time.

And as I watched them standing there, looking so complete, I realized our family sessions with the Dr. Phil wannabe probably weren't as stupid as they seemed.

That day, right after I said good-bye to Marc, I walked into the house, only to find both my parents sitting in the living room, totally hysterically panicked, with the cops well on their way.

Apparently my mom called a bunch of times, just wanting to check in and see how I was feeling. But when I failed to answer she grew concerned and came straight home to find an empty house and no note.

Well, naturally she assumed something horrible had happened, since Zoë's murder pretty much guaranteed that we'll never reside in that safe, protective bubble again. And so she called my dad, and he notified the police, and then they both sat in the den, waiting for the other shoe to drop.

I felt awful that I'd put them into such a panic, and it took me awhile to calm them down, but when I did finally get a chance to explain, I made sure to tell them only what they needed to know, while preserving the rest for Marc, Zoë, and me.

Then I reached into my pocket and handed over the tape (making no mention of the diary), while cautioning them about what it most likely contained. Then I sank onto the couch in total exhaustion, relieved to let them take over and handle these things for a change.

I also explained how the way we were living was no longer working, and how I needed them to finally figure things out. Because while all the late nights and fights would never bring Zoë back, they would eventually destroy what little we had left.

Zoë's killer was recently convicted. Apparently he'd made a longtime habit of targeting small-town girls with big dreams, promising the moon before taking their lives. Seven victims later and the creep still didn't even own a camera. And the Web page he'd set up was a total fake.

But the good news is he'll never see daylight again. He'll never be able to betray someone's faith, the way he did with Zoë.

And as for Jason? Well, the charges are all lined up, with separate trials for the drugs, the videos, and the underage girls. And with such a strong case against him, they won't have to rely on Carly and Zoë to convict him.

Still, pretty much everybody around here knows, and the gossip is worse than ever. But I no longer care. I'm just glad I didn't lose my best friends, Abby and Jenay, and was even lucky enough to find some new ones in Marc and Teresa.

Jenay showed up at Zoë's party with Chess. And Abby, having decided that her nerves and self-consciousness were solely to blame for their awkward first kiss, showed up with Jax. And after seeing how good they are together, how truly well matched they are, I'm glad she ignored my bad advice and decided to give him another chance.

Parker came too, only he brought his new girlfriend, Heidi. And even though things are still a little uncomfortable between us, I was glad he made it.

And when Teresa walked up alone, everyone turned and stared. But since I know full well what it's like to be the center of unwanted attention, I waved her over and told her to join us.

She and Sean broke up, like the second the story broke. And her parents were so angry at what she'd done and the danger she'd put herself in, and yet hugely relieved that she'd made it out basically unharmed, that they went out and bought her a brand-new car—a black BMW, loaded with the most modern GPS tracking system so they can monitor her every move. Even though, technically, she's not even old enough to drive it yet.

And after Paula passed out little Baggies full of Wonder bread, and Abby and Jenay lit the candles, Carly tried to read a poem she wrote especially for my sister, only she had to stop halfway through when she broke down in tears.

Just a few days after the whole Jason story leaked, she showed up at our house, begging our forgiveness, unwilling to leave until she was convinced that she had it. But she and I are okay now. I mean, we're not exactly friends, but now we can at least say hey when we see each other at school.

Then Marc docked his iPod and turned up the sound, and everyone gathered around the new bench, Marc on my left, my parents on my right, as we listened to Coltrane, tossed crumbs to those fat, greedy ducks, and remembered Zoë.